PRAISE FOR NIK JAMES NOVELS

About *HIGH COUNTRY JUSTICE*

"Caleb Marlowe is handsome, honest, loyal, fearless and strong enough to wrestle a cougar. He's also an appealing character and bound to be popular with readers....

The story is filled with heinous outlaws, plenty of shootouts, heroic acts and twists and turns. The stage-coach robbers are not your average bunch of outlaws. The ending is a nice surprise..."

— Barbara Ellis, *The Denver Post*

"I have not read a good Western for a while and this one really hit the spot. It took me back to the days I would borrow books from my father that were written by Zane Grey, Louis Lamour, Max Brand and other authors that he had collected and treasured enough to keep on his shelves. This book has the feel of those old time favorites and took me back in time...."

— Cathy Geha, GoodReads Review

"AN EXCELLENT READ! I love a good western and that's what this was, a really good western. It had all the elements. A dangerous small town filled with down and out of luck silver miners whose mines were played out. A shifty-eyed sheriff and trouble....

Reading a Nik James book is like watching a movie. The description of the country as well as their crafting of characters made everything as clear as watching it..."

— Long and Short Reviews

———

About *SILVER AND BULLETS*

"Refreshing.... A timely addition to the Western canon."

— Sarah Steers, ALA *Booklist* Review

NOVELS BY MAY McGOLDRICK

16th CENTURY HIGHLANDER NOVELS

A Midsummer Wedding *(novella)*
The Thistle and the Rose

Macpherson Brothers Trilogy
Angel of Skye (Book 1)
Heart of Gold (Book 2)
Beauty of the Mist (Book 3)
Macpherson Trilogy (Box Set)
The Intended
Flame
Tess and the Highlander

Highland Treasure Trilogy
The Dreamer (Book 1)
The Enchantress (Book 2)
The Firebrand (Book 3)
Highland Treasure Trilogy Box Set

Scottish Relic Trilogy
Much Ado About Highlanders (Book 1)
Taming the Highlander (Book 2)
Tempest in the Highlands (Book 3)

Scottish Relic Trilogy Box Set

Love and Mayhem

18th CENTURY NOVELS

Secret Vows
The Promise (Pennington Family)
The Rebel
Secret Vows Box Set

Scottish Dream Trilogy (Pennington Family)
Borrowed Dreams (Book 1)
Captured Dreams (Book 2)
Dreams of Destiny (Book 3)
Scottish Dream Trilogy Box Set

REGENCY & 19th CENTURY NOVELS

Pennington Regency-Era Series
Romancing the Scot
It Happened in the Highlands
Sweet Home Highland Christmas *(novella)*
Sleepless in Scotland
Dearest Millie *(novella)*
How to Ditch a Duke *(novella)*

The Prince in the Pantry (*novella*)

Royal Highlander Series
Highland Crown
Highland Jewel
Highland Sword

Ghost of the Thames

CONTEMPORARY ROMANCE

Thanksgiving in Connecticut
Made in Heaven

————

NONFICTION

Marriage of Minds: Collaborative Writing
Step Write Up: Writing Exercises for 21st Century

THE WINTER ROAD

CALEB MARLOWE SERIES

NIK JAMES

MM BOOKS

Thank you for choosing this book. In the event that you appreciate this book, please consider sharing the good word(s) by leaving a review, or connect with the author.

Edited by Cyrus McGoldrick

Cover by Dar Albert, at WickedSmartDesigns.com

1

The Rocky Mountains, Colorado
September 1877

THE GROUND RUMBLED BENEATH HER. A cracking noise,
sharp and loud and sudden, echoed off the high walls of
the mountain pass. Nell Cody squeezed her eyes shut
beneath the blanket.

Another nightmare. She'd had plenty of them since
they left Boulder.

All day long, the clouds had hung over the wagon
train, heavy with rain. It was as if the sky wanted to cry
but couldn't. It didn't dare.

Just like her.

Nell was sick at heart for the life they'd left behind. Their house, their neighbors, her school, her friends. She yearned for them. Most important of all, she bled inside for the lost connection with her late mother. She'd never again experience the sensation she felt whenever she stepped up onto the front porch, saw her mother's empty rocking chair, and felt her presence.

She was not just there. She was everywhere—in the walls, the furniture, even in the scented air of their house—enshrined by Nell's cherished memories of her.

Her mother was dead three years now. Gone in the eyes of the world. But Nell knew her sweet soul had remained in that house to watch over her.

Nell was angry with her father for uprooting them the way he did. John Cody was a pastor. He had a respected church in Boulder. A growing flock of followers. But then, seemingly overnight, he'd become obsessed with moving to Youngblood Creek.

So here they were, traveling with four other families. Altogether, fourteen souls in wagons on their way to an outpost of a town in the mountains far to the west of Boulder.

What did she know of this frontier? Very little, other than stories she'd heard. The cruelty of an unforgiving Nature. The ever-present threats of violence from roving bands of Arapaho and Cheyenne who had not yet given up their fight, refusing to go north to the new reservations.

And what had she been told of the town they were moving to? Nothing. Only that they didn't even have a church or a school. Her father and some others had to raise money to build them.

What had she done to deserve such a fate?

Nell was fifteen. She was well-read and well-taught. And she was already old enough to have plans of her own. She'd decided that she would teach after finishing school. In a few years, she'd marry and settle near her father. In Boulder. But now she was traveling through a wilderness to a place she knew nothing about. *Nothing.*

Frustrated and unable to sleep, she'd moved her bedding from the wagon in the middle of the night and spread it on the ground between the wheels. The stony hardness and the dampness beneath her only reinforced her mood. They never should have come on this trip. She should have fought harder.

Instead, she had to endure endless days of travel... and nights filled with foul dreams.

The crack and *twang* of more gunfire erupted somewhere nearby, and the acrid smell of gun smoke pinched her senses. Nell sat bolt upright. This was no nightmare.

"Nell?" Her father's voice rang out from above. "Where are you?"

"Down here."

A horse thundered past their wagon, and the rider didn't slow down as he fired two shots through the canvas.

"Stay where you are."

These attackers were not Arapaho or Cheyenne. In the dim light of the dying fire, four white men spurred their sweating mounts back and forth across the center of the camp, pouring bullets into the canopies.

Return fire flashed from one of the wagons, then another.

A wave as cold as ice washed down Nell's back. Fear kept her frozen in place for a few seconds. But her mind ordered her to move. She had to help her people. She'd learned to shoot when she was still a girl, but she'd left her gun belt in the wagon.

Her father's rifle barked above her. Shouts and screams, nearly drowned out by the crackle of gunfire, filled the smoky air.

Tonight, they'd stopped and set up camp a good hour before the sun set. It was earlier than usual. But Bart Kelly, their guide, said this was a fine place to stop, and they'd drawn the five wagons into a circle for safety.

He knew these mountains. He'd led many parties of travelers west.

A cry rang out from the wagon next to theirs. Someone inside had been hit in the brewer's wagon, and she saw him jump out, raising his shotgun toward the attackers. Before he could shoot, however, a rider wheeled and fired. The man sank to his knees.

"Papa, throw the gun belt down."

The killer dug his spurs into his horse's flanks and was gone.

"Papa!" she yelled louder. "My gun."

In front of her, the belt with the Colt Peacemaker dropped into the dirt. Reaching out, she grabbed hold of it and dragged it back under the wagon, where she strapped it around her waist.

Just then, the brewer's wife ran out to her fallen husband, screaming at the blackguards. The woman reached for the shotgun, but another outlaw shot first. The bullet knocked her back on her haunches.

Nell stared in horror for only a moment before scurrying out from beneath the wagon.

"*Get back.*" Her father's voice boomed in the night.

The wounded woman slumped into her arms as Nell reached her. A shot thudded into the ground inches from her knee.

"Move. Fast. Get under the wagon."

Her father continued to shoot, giving Nell the chance she needed. She dragged the older woman back and managed to pull her beneath the wagon. Her eyes were open, but only for a moment. The light in them faded and disappeared. She was gone.

Anger flooded through Nell, and she yanked the Colt from its holster.

A fellow traveler dashed out from between two wagons and jumped at one of the riders, his hands clamping on to the man's arm. The outlaw never hesitated, shooting him point-blank.

The rider raced across the opening, taking aim at another wagon. Nell fired at the killer, knocking his hat from his head as the bullet went high, and he veered off.

"They've got us. We have no chance."

Her father's despairing voice caused her anger to rise like bile into her throat. *He'd* done this. It was because of him that they were here.

"Nell, I need you to take my bag and run."

The money, of course. Always the promise of a greener pasture. It was on John Cody's advice that these families uprooted their lives. It was because of him that they were traveling to Youngblood Creek. Every one of these people was a parishioner from her father's church.

"Do you hear me?"

She heard him, but she couldn't tear her eyes from

the bloodbath before her. No one in their group was a match for what they were facing. One by one, she saw her fellow travelers fall. Already, the camp was littered with bodies.

"You have to go now. Get far enough from the wagons where they won't find you. They can't know how many we are. They won't know you're missing."

Fourteen of them had left Boulder, including Mr. Kelly. Her gaze raked the open space, searching for their guide. Where *was* Kelly? He was a hunter. Their best shot. The one responsible for getting them through this wilderness.

"Folks are relying on us in Youngblood Creek. You've *got* to make it there."

"They are relying on you. *You!*" she shouted back. "You want to fulfill your promise? Then you come with me."

Nell was angry with her father, but she would not go without him.

Reality stared her in the face. He was all she had. The only parent she had left. And he was not the one who was taking innocent lives. Even though he'd made the wrongheaded decision to leave Boulder, it was not his fault that they'd come under attack. In his heart John Cody was a good man, an honest man. He cared for his flock. But the cost of his error was so high. Nell's eyes blurred as they took in the bloody scene before her.

An old man sat upright against the water barrel she'd helped him fill at the creek before supper. His blank and lifeless eyes were fixed on the body of his fallen son. The printer and his wife—so proud of the press they had boxed up in their wagon—both lay dead. The husband and wife excited to start farming lay in a heap in the dirt.

But where was Kelly?

Suddenly, a hand grasped Nell's arm. Before she could react, she was dragged out into the darkness behind the wagon. Her father. His rifle was smoking in one hand. His eyes bore into hers.

"Did you hear what I said?"

"Your promise. Your mission. I heard. But you have to go with me."

"They'll see us escape. They'll kill us both. I'll distract them while you get away." He snatched a leather bag the size of a brick from the front of the wagon and stuffed it into her hand. "Take this, Nell. Go into the trees. Hide."

"I'm not going without you."

"Youngblood Creek. Please, Nell. Promise me that you'll get it to them. Lives depend on it."

"Do you see all the dead around us? Was this

worth it?"

"Don't. We have no time for this now. But please promise me that you'll get this money to the people in that town. They expect it. They've been waiting for it."

Before she could reply, a shot rang out behind her, and her father's eyes opened wide. His hand went to his heart, and she saw blood seeping through his fingers.

"*NO!*" she cried out.

As he collapsed at her feet, she turned. Not a dozen paces from them, the hatless blackguard was striding toward her. Before he could take three more steps, Nell raised her pistol and fired.

The man went down and lay still. Her breath caught in her chest. She'd killed a man. But she'd do it again if she had to.

"Papa, let's go." She sank to her knees. Her father's eyes were open. She shook him. Touched his face. Tugged on his arm. "We can make it. You and me. We'll go to Youngblood Creek. Please, get up."

Tears rushed down her face. Sobs choked her. She knew her words were useless. He wasn't moving. He wasn't breathing.

He was all she had, and she'd been so angry with him. And now he lay dead.

"You can't do this to me. You can't leave me."

Nell didn't know how long she knelt beside his body,

but suddenly she was aware that the guns had fallen silent. The echoes faded away, and an eerie quiet claimed the mountain pass.

Was she the last one left?

One of the bandits called out from the center of the encampment. She wiped the tears off her face and peered under the wagon at them. They were reloading their revolvers. Bodies of her fellow travelers lay strewn about the camp like discarded firewood. All dead.

The killers wore bandanas around their necks, but they hadn't even tried to hide their faces. They'd meant to murder everyone all along.

She recognized a voice, and the last of her hope withered. Bart Kelly—the guide they'd trusted to take them safely to the mountain town of Youngblood Creek —strode to the center of the group, brandishing his rifle.

"Go find Cody." He motioned toward their wagon.

Nell couldn't move. A cold stillness, a feeling of numbness, seeped through her, but she knew she couldn't give in to it.

Reaching down, she closed her father's eyes. "I promise. I'll get this to Youngblood Creek for you."

Forcing herself to move, she slid the pistol into its holster, picked up the rifle, and disappeared into the darkness.

2
————————

Three months later
December 1877

HENRY JORDAN REINED in the dark bay gelding, unfastened the front of his elkskin coat, and loosened the leather thong on his Colt Peacemaker.

He'd seen no sign of human life in two days. And he didn't see any now. Only trees, high rock walls, and the five burned out hulks of wagons in front of him. The charred remains stood out starkly against the glistening white of the foot-deep snow.

On both sides of him, all the way up to the base of the bluffs lining the pass, forests of pine and spruce were pockmarked with groves of leafless aspen. A black creek down a hill from the destroyed camp was lined with cottonwood and scrub pine. Only the occasional chirp of a bird or *chit, chit, chit* of a squirrel broke the silence. And, of course, the moan of ever-present wind through the trees.

Overall, though, it was quiet as a grave here.

"Fitting. Eh, big fella?"

The gelding's ears flicked back at Henry, but he said nothing in response.

Henry's first thought was that this looked to be the work of Cheyenne raiders. It had been a year and a half since Custer got his ass kicked back in Wyoming. Since then, the army had made it their mission to wipe out any tribe that had a hand in the battle. And any tribe that hadn't, for that matter. As a result, the Indians only got angrier. To the north, it was largely Lakota and some Arapaho who were still running and fighting. Down here, Cheyenne.

Henry had fought them for two years. He wasn't given much choice, being conscripted to serve. Many young men of his mother's people had voluntarily joined the white soldiers to fight the Sioux. After all, they'd been the enemies of the Crow for generations. But his Irish father had raised him as a white man after his mother died. No one knew where Henry's loyalties lay. The army knew nothing of his parentage.

All ancient history now. He was on the trail to a new life.

But these travelers had clearly had no chance.

What lay before him was a massacre. He felt some hesitation about riding into the circle of the wagons. What exactly had happened to these people? Had their blood been shed suddenly? Their scalps taken? Their bodies left for the wolves and coyotes and other scavengers to drag off into the forest?

No human remains pushed up through the powdery shroud of snow. Henry hoped for their sakes that death had come quickly.

He nudged his mount toward the closest wagon. Pulling off a glove, he broke off a piece of burnt wood from a sideboard. He figured the attack had come late summer or early fall. The rains and the snow had done little so far to scour the wood clean.

One of the wagons had collapsed under the weight of its load, and the remains of some kind of machine had tumbled out onto the ground. A printing press. Pieces of it had melted and twisted from the heat.

These folks had been looking for a new life, the same as he was. With any luck Henry's friend Caleb Marlowe was already in Denver waiting for him.

When he'd first met Marlowe up in Wyoming, they were both nearing the end of their hitches with the army. Henry knew him right off. Marlowe was legendary as a scout long before the army roped him in to work for them. He'd ridden for years with none other than Old Jake Bell, who was as knowledgeable about the frontier as any man alive. It was said that the two of them had explored every inch of the West from the Missouri to Mormon country, and from the Bighorn Mountains to the Calabasas. Before Old Jake retired to a farm someplace back East, they'd blazed trails to the Montana goldfields and served as guides for miners and homesteaders up and down the Rockies. Later, while Henry was finishing up his time with the army, Marlowe had taken a badge in Greeley, and his lightning-fast draw and deadly aim had only added to the legend.

All that didn't stop Henry and Marlowe from raising hell and forming a fast friendship, though. He was a good man—brave as any Crow war chief, solid and tough as hickory—and the two of them now had plans to go partners on a ranch down near the silver boomtown of Elkhorn. If things went accordingly, some cattle-raising, some prospecting, maybe even a wife and children lay ahead for Henry. A settled life in one place. A man could hope, anyway.

But these folks had hopes too, he thought, looking

around him. Wherever they'd come from, Henry could imagine them loading up their earthly possessions and turning their eyes westward. They were going to a place where they hoped to put down roots and build something fresh and lasting for themselves and their families.

Except they didn't make it.

He rode slowly from wagon to wagon, feeling a tightness in his throat as he looked into them.

A hint of the acrid smell of burnt belongings was still present. Crates and trunks had been opened and the contents dumped out before the fires started. In the corner of one wagon, there were shattered bits of blue and white dinner plates, decorated with birds and flowers. Perhaps they'd been a wedding gift to a young couple. In another corner, charred scraps of wool and calico, mostly covered by snow, fluttered in the breeze.

All dead. Gone from this world into the next. There was nothing *he* could do to help them.

Henry started to turn his gelding's head south, and paused. Something down by the ice-lined creek caught his eye. Leaving the circle of wagons, he urged his horse down the hill.

Dismounting, he pulled his Winchester '73 from its scabbard and approached the neat row of snowy mounds.

There were a dozen, at least. Rocks protruded from

the snow. They'd been piled up over graves that he figured were fairly shallow. Some of the stones had been scattered, no doubt by scavengers scratching to get underneath, but it appeared the animals had given up and moved on to easier pickings.

Only the grave at the end was marked. A rude cross made of sticks was stuck into the mound, and something at the base of the cross drew Henry's eye. Going down on one knee, he brushed away the snow that covered it.

There, positioned between a pair of rocks, was a Bible.

3

A CHILL WASHED down Nell's back, and the hatchet hung suspended in her hand, ready to strike. She held her breath and listened. A snuffle of a horse? The cold December wind whispered through the tops of the spruce trees. Some of the cottonwood branches she'd dragged out from the forest lay in a pile at her feet.

She could see nothing on either side of the nearly frozen river in the valley below. Nothing but tawny grass pushing up through the snow.

The cabin was situated in a protected notch of a rocky rise. Cliffs that rose nearly fifty feet on either side bordered a steep, boulder-filled hill. The creek tumbled down through a series of falls and eventually joined the river in the valley.

The opening through the tall spruce trees provided a view of anyone approaching.

The sound didn't come again.

The past three months had been hell, and this was exactly the reason why. Phantom sounds. Imaginary shadows. Not once since the slaughter of her father and the others had she been able to relax. She was alone in the middle of the wilderness, far from anything resembling civilization, with no idea how to get back to where she'd come from or where she had to go.

She glanced at the smoke curling above the chimney of the cabin thirty paces away.

Abandoned by someone else, but a life saver for her. A place she'd decided to spend the winter. Finding it was a miracle.

The night Bart Kelly and his gang murdered her father and the others, she ran blindly through the forest. She suspected they'd come after her. The fear of the outlaws and the wild animals pushed her. Her chest burned. She recalled the branches whipping her and cutting her face. She didn't know how long or how far she ran. Only when she found herself standing in the chilly shallows of a river did she stop. Feelings of loss enclosed her like a death shroud. In those moments, when the will to survive was fading, she remembered the promise she'd made to her father. She had a job to do. There were people in Youngblood Creek who relied on her.

Putting one foot in front of the other, Nell followed a stream up a rise. As the moon rose above the black tree-tops, she stumbled upon a low-roofed cabin. It was empty and cold, but the walls themselves were an unexpected gift.

Three months had passed. Three months of learning how to survive.

Nell turned back to her chore and chopped a piece from the cottonwood. As she yanked the hatchet free and lifted it in the air again, she heard the crack of wood breaking. Someone was here. And close.

In her first dark days in the cabin, she'd prayed to hear the sound of horses and the rumble and rattle and squeak of wagons. But she was plenty old enough to understand the reality of her situation. She was fifteen. A woman. To most of the men who would be passing through these mountains, she'd be prey.

Hatchet in hand, she scooped up her gun belt from the branch and sprinted toward the log cabin.

As she ran, she glanced back over her shoulder, down through the opening the creek had carved between the trees. Whoever was there, he was still not in sight.

At the rear of the cabin, Nell strapped on the gun

belt and scrambled up the notched tree trunk that served as a ladder to the nearly flat roof. She crept to the front edge.

She laid the hatchet in the snow next to the broken axe handle she'd left up here. She drew her Peacemaker from its holster and cocked it.

The breeze shifted, blowing smoke from the stone chimney into her face and stinging her eyes. Whoever was coming would know someone was living in the cabin. They wouldn't just go by. Not in the middle of winter.

The horse and rider appeared in the valley below, close to the line of spruce trees. It took only a moment before the man saw the cabin. He stared up at it for a long while.

"You're not welcome here," she whispered. "Keep going."

Nell's heart dropped when he turned his mount and began the climb toward the cabin. As he came up the hill, she looked hard at him, trying to decide what to do. She was no cold-blooded killer. But after the attack on the wagon train, she would never let herself be a victim again.

He was wearing a heavy leather coat and a black, flat-brimmed hat. Her gaze took in the large bearskin rolled up behind him and the rifle in the saddle scabbard.

He had a horse. And for Nell to have a chance of finding her way to any town, she'd need something she could ride.

The Colt was heavy, and the grip was cool in her hand. Edging back a little to be sure she was out of sight, she listened as he drew closer.

The thud and crunch of hooves in the snow grew louder.

"Hullo," the rider called out. "Saw the cabin and wanted to stop."

The sound of him reining in reached Nell's ears. She stayed silent and still.

"Anyone at home? If you're in there, I'm just passing and mean no harm."

Silence.

"Say the word if you want me to keep going."

She could imagine the man sitting in the saddle, his gaze moving from the closed door of the cabin to the chimney smoke to the fresh kindling and the stack of firewood.

"All right then," he called out. "I'm climbing down. Don't shoot."

The squeak of saddle leather was followed by his

boots crunching on the snow. He stood still for a long time, and Nell barely took a breath. As he moved toward the door a few steps, she inched up to where she could see the top of his black hat. He was very tall and broad across the shoulders. The brim of his hat covered his eyes.

She laid the barrel of the six-gun on her left forearm to steady it and aimed directly below the hat. All she had to do was squeeze the trigger and the danger would be behind her.

He went to the door. He was directly below her. He knocked.

"Anyone in there?"

Silence. Her hand remained steady.

"Coming in."

He was a dead man. Her finger tightened on the trigger.

"I came by them graves near the burnt wagons. I'm thinking you buried them folks. I paid my respects."

Nell eased off the trigger. Putting the pistol down, her fingers closed around the axe handle instead, and she swung the weapon as hard as she could in a swift downward arc.

The blow landed solidly. That wide-brimmed hat offered no protection.

Nell heard the grunt as the man went down, but she

didn't wait to see the results. Picking up her gun, she pointed it over the edge of the roof.

The man was sprawled flat on his belly. His booted legs stuck out the door. He wasn't moving or making a sound.

"You just saved your own life," she murmured. "For now, anyway."

4

HENRY SMELLED RABBIT.

When he tried to blink his eyes open, a white-hot poker stabbed through his brain from temple to temple.

He took a breath, tried to pry them open again, and immediately became conscious of two things. First, he was lying on a cold dirt floor. Second, a herd of buffalo the size of Montana was stampeding through his head. Very painful.

Making a valiant attempt to push at least one eye open, he tried to sit up. That was when he became aware of a third thing. He was trussed up like a hog waiting for slaughter.

Some low-down, no-account skunk had tied him up.

Ignoring the pain as best he could, Henry wormed his

way toward the closest wall, but only moved an inch or so before the back of his head bumped hard against a rough log. Instantly, two of those buffalo bulls who'd taken up residence in his head came together with a tremendous crash of horns. Stars exploded in his face, blinding him.

Slowly, it all came back to him. The burnt wagons, the graves.

In the nearly frozen mud along the creek by the graves, he'd seen small footprints. He'd decided they belonged to a woman or a boy.

At the site of the massacre, the same boot tracks had come and gone a number of times. It hadn't been difficult following them. They led down the creek to a long wide valley. From there, the trail followed the line of trees. After less than an hour of riding, he'd reached another stream that tumbled down from the hills. It was there that Henry had seen a cabin with smoke coming from a chimney.

The question went through his mind about who was living there. The cabin, with its stone chimney, was too permanent to be a miner's shack. Those fellows threw up the simplest of shelters, worked their claim, and then moved on. Besides, there was no busted, discarded equipment like the long-toms or sieves used for separating the gravel from gold. And this was no homesteader's place, either. It was too high in the mountains to grow much of anything.

A trapper or a hunter, he'd decided, spotting what looked like racks for cleaning and stretching hides by the creek. But there was no sign of any horses or mules that a hunter would need for transporting his merchandise. And they were a hell of a long way from any towns.

As he'd ridden up the hill, he'd seen more of the same footprints. Maybe the trapper had a wife or a boy. Henry didn't feel too worried about approaching. They'd probably be happy to hear another human voice.

He blinked and tried to clear his head. What happened after that was a little murky, but he tried to piece it together.

He'd gotten down from his horse, done his damnedest to let whoever was inside know that he meant no harm. Then *wham*! He never heard the varmint sneaking up on him.

Henry pulled at the leather thongs binding his wrists behind his back but only managed to feel them cutting into him. The sonovabitch had done a fine job of it, taking his boots and tying his ankles and knees tight, as well.

He lifted his head and looked around the cabin. There was a small fire on a stone hearth. Dim light came in through uncaulked gaps in the log walls and through one small window with a piece of deerskin hanging over it. Still day. He couldn't have been out too long.

The cabin's contents were spare, to say the least. A small, charred trunk for a seat by the fire. Some half-burnt canvas on a pile of meadow grass in one corner. The skins from a few small animals were rolled up on the dirt floor near the bedding. A scorched keg, a ladle, a tin cup, and a chipped bowl. That was all.

One person lived here.

From a cooking pot on the hearth came the rabbit smell.

He heard footsteps, and the door swung open, bringing in a blast of cold. Henry closed his eyes, pretending he was still unconscious. His captor stood for a long moment on the threshold and then moved across to the fire.

Light steps. No one else followed. No conversations. An armful of wood dropped onto the packed dirt.

He opened his eyes to see someone feeding branches into the fire.

Small. Thin. An oversized black wool coat, tan wool pants, and a black hat with a three inch brim. A gun belt worn over the coat. Considering how he'd handled Henry, tough and smart.

It was only when the man picked up the ladle and

stirred the pot that Henry saw the face. *A woman.* He was more than a little surprised. Henry was over six feet, and she'd taken him down like a straw dog.

This was one story that he wouldn't be telling anytime soon.

He stared at her profile. She was pretty enough, with regular features. Straight black hair was fastened into a single braid that disappeared into the collar of the coat.

Still crouching by the fire, she shot a quick look at Henry and saw him watching her. She came to her feet fast, one hand on the iron she wore on her hip. They stared at each other for a long time until she broke the silence.

"About time you woke up."

"Considering the way my head feels, I'm surprised I woke up at all."

"Who are you?" they both asked at the same time.

"I ask the questions."

She had a point. Henry was tied up, and she now held the gun. The brighter side of that coin was that he was alive. She had his horse and his weapons and all the gear he'd been traveling with, including the back pay he'd received when he left the army. If she meant to kill him, he'd already be dead.

"Who are you?" she asked again.

"Henry Jordan, recently Sergeant Henry Jordan of the 3rd Cavalry."

"A deserter?"

"Discharged. My papers are in my saddlebags, if you want to see them."

"What are you doing here?"

"I'm on my way to Denver."

The muzzle of the six-gun lifted until Henry was looking straight down the barrel. He hadn't answered her question.

"I saw the burnt wagons down the valley. You buried all them folks, didn't you?"

She said nothing. The gun was still pointed at his head.

"Your footprints were all around it. I tracked you here."

"Why?"

"I thought you were a kid. I was worried."

She snorted. The Colt lowered a fraction of an inch.

"That's what folks do, traveling in these mountains. They come upon a cabin or a camp, and they stop by and say hullo. Most like to see others. To trade and barter. Share a meal and the news of the world. Then the travelers get back on the road."

She hesitated for a moment and then pouched the

six-gun. Pulling off her hat, she hung it on a peg on the wall.

Henry was tired of looking up at her from the floor. Edging back to the wall, he levered himself up into a sitting position, and she watched him do it.

"A sad sight, those burnt wagons."

No response.

"You know who did it?"

He might as well have been having this conversation with the wall, as she offered no reply.

"That attack didn't come from any Indian raiding party."

Her head turned, and he held her gaze.

"I suspect white men did that."

Henry was good with people. Even better with women. He understood their moods. What made them angry and frustrated. What made them happy. Over the years he'd developed a reputation for it. Right now, it wasn't difficult to sense the sadness in her.

"The frontier is filled with stories of outlaws. The varmints rob stagecoaches, mining claims, an occasional bank, and now they even go after trains." He had no idea what happened down there. Still, she was listening. "When I was up in Montana, I heard about home-steaders or miners paying a guide to take them through mountains or Indian country, only to have that villain's gang waiting to bushwhack them when they were out in the wilderness."

She watched him in silence.

"When did it happen? In the fall?"

"September."

Henry was surprised that she answered, but the pieces fell together. It all made sense. The cabin. The graves. The back-and-forth trek down the creek. She hadn't been living here too long. She would have been traveling with the wagon train. Somehow, she'd escaped the fate of the others and had been living here since.

"That was mighty brave of you to go back there and do what you did."

She crouched down by the fire and stirred the pot.

"What's your name?"

Silence.

"Let me say it again, miss. I mean you no harm. I'm only passing through. You don't have to be afraid of me."

"Nell. Nell Cody."

"How old are you, Miss Cody?"

"Fifteen."

Too young to be on her own. It was a miracle she'd survived this long. "And your people were among those you buried?"

The nod was barely noticeable. His heart sank for her, for what she must have gone through. He had dozens of questions, but he doubted she'd answer any of them.

"Hungry?" she asked, looking over at him.

"Starving."

Without another word, she drew a knife from her belt, padded across the floor, and cut the leather bonds.

5

THE SKY WAS iron gray and low enough for Henry to reach up and punch a hole in it. Not a good-looking day for travel, but it wasn't snowing. And tomorrow might not be better. Or the day after. Winter was here.

Yesterday, while Henry was unconscious, Nell had fed and watered the gelding and tethered him around the side of the cabin. From the disarray in his saddle-bags, he figured she'd seen his papers. She knew who he was before they talked. Her questions had been a test. He'd passed.

Henry walked over and fussed with a hobble strap on his saddle while he studied her across the open space by the woodpile. She was busy chopping firewood with a hatchet. If she'd had a mind to do it, she could have taken his horse and been long gone from here. But she didn't.

After she cut the ropes off him, he'd tried to talk to her as they ate. Put her mind at ease. She was a person of very few words, even worse than Marlowe. It was obvious to Henry that she still didn't trust him.

Folks who survived the kind of mess she'd experienced generally wanted to talk about it, he'd found. They needed a listening ear. So he'd asked about the people who were on the wagon train and who she'd lost. No answer. He asked who attacked them. No answer. He asked where the wagons came from and where they were heading.

She'd answered that one. The wagon train had started off from Boulder. They were going to Youngblood Creek.

Henry knew of Youngblood Creek, but he'd never been there. It was a solid week's ride west of Denver in good weather. Like many other towns in Colorado, the original hope of finding gold there had quickly disappeared. Word was, however, that it had a protected valley where farming was possible. It was actually one of the places he and Marlowe had considered settling, but they'd decided against it.

With what was left of their money once they bought

land, their plan was to raise cattle and feed nearby miners and townsfolk. Elkhorn had plenty. Youngblood Creek, not so.

The wind was cold and coming out of the northwest, and Henry caught the smell of snow in the air. The day was wasting away. His partner was waiting for him in Denver. He needed to get on the trail.

His eyes drifted to Nell. The hatchet rose and fell, splintering the wood.

Damn it, he couldn't just leave her here.

Last night, he offered to take her with him. He explained that they could ride together most of the way and work their way south until they reached the wagon road that went through Berthold's Pass. They'd be able to get her a horse of her own there. After that, it would be a relatively easy ride from there to Denver.

Even though she wouldn't tell him what family she lost or whether she had any kin left, to his thinking the city would provide a chance for her to find help.

Her reply was curt. No. She wasn't going to Denver. She was going to Youngblood Creek.

And when he asked her how she planned to get there, the expression on her face said it all. Raised eyebrows, pointed look. She expected him to take her. But that didn't work for him, and he told her so. He wasn't adding a week or more onto his trip. He was going to Denver. Besides, if she went with him, she'd surely be able to find folks heading out that way come spring.

No. She'd wait *here* 'til spring.

He'd argued that it would be damn foolhardy staying here alone.

She'd quoted some Scripture at him next. *Ye shall be scattered, every man to his own, and shall leave me alone: and yet I am not alone.*

That ended their conversation.

Henry ran a hand down his face and shook his head at the stubborn young woman across the way. The wind cut around the cabin and sliced through him. He guessed she'd never spent a winter in the high country. She had no way of knowing, but these were months that could kill even the most experienced mountain men. Blizzards came so fast and hard and fierce that a person could get lost and freeze to death not ten feet from shelter. On top of that, being so completely isolated during the long dark season ahead could drive anyone out of their mind.

There were so many other dangers that he could and should have reminded her about last night. Like the bears and wolves and cougars that would happily make a meal of her.

Beyond all that, however, there was an even worse kind of danger. The human kind.

He caught her watching him. This morning, he'd announced he was leaving. She'd said good riddance.

And yet, he was still standing here.

"Hell, who am I kidding?"

Henry fastened the front of his elkskin coat and tugged on his gloves and crunched through the snow toward her.

She only glanced up at him for a moment before continuing to chop away at the wood.

"I'm leaving."

A chunk of wood flew off and dropped into the snow by his boot. He stooped, picked it up, and turned it over his hands.

"But before I go, I want you to hear me out."

"We're done talking."

"You might be, but I'm not."

She'd been out here three months and had survived just fine. And she hadn't seen a human face before his. That gave her false confidence.

"You might not think so, but this cabin of yours would be tough to defend in a real fight."

"I did well enough with you."

"I was one man. And I didn't come looking for trouble." He looked up at the cliffs rising above the cabin and at the thick forest of spruce and pine. "If some mangy cur passed by, and he had two or three more mangy curs with him, they'd scout out this place. They wouldn't come traipsing right up to your door."

She paused, the hatchet poised by her ear. "I knew you were coming before you showed up."

"Listen to what I'm saying. I was one man with no intention of doing you any harm. I smelled the smoke from your chimney from way down the valley. I wanted to be seen."

He didn't want to say the words. Rape and murder were not uncommon out here, and she wouldn't stand a chance.

The edge of the tool bit sharply into the wood again.

"Come with me."

"No." Chop. Another piece of wood dropped to the ground.

"You can't stay here on your own."

Nell gave no sign that she was still listening. The hatchet rose and fell, deepening the notch.

Henry took a breath, trying to keep the growing annoyance out of his voice. "You're fifteen. Alone. There are dangers in these mountains that'll kill you, sure as we're standing here."

Silence.

"The bodies you buried down there." He motioned

in the general direction of the massacre. "I'm sure there are grown men in them graves. They're dead now. They couldn't protect themselves, never mind their families. Not one of them survived. What makes you think you can make it on your own? And out here, there's no one to help you."

The tool's edge bit deep once again.

Annoyance turned into a flash of anger. Reaching over, he yanked the hatchet from her hand and threw it into the snow ten feet away.

In an instant, she was up, and the Colt was pointed at his chest. He could have knocked it out of her hand, tied her to his horse, and forced her to go with him to Denver. Henry was worried enough to do that. But he'd rather she saw reason and decide to do the right thing on her own.

"You've *got* to be reasonable," he barked.

"What gives you the right to—"

He cut her off. "I know these mountains. I been through here before. That valley down there is a natural trail for buffalo. And I'd wager you've already seen them."

She glared at him and said nothing.

"The Arapaho have always hunted here. The government has elbowed them onto reservation land up in Wyoming, but there's more than a few of them left."

She'd ignored his lectures about the dangers of the winter and outlaws. But he was going to make sure she heard the rest.

"There's a whole passel of Cheyenne who have migrated this way. When they're not fighting the army, both tribes are following the buffalo herds."

Henry jerked a thumb toward the cabin.

"The trapper who lived here might have been on good terms with the Arapaho, but those days are over. The US Government has seen to that. My guess is that's why he cleared out."

Nell frowned but she slid the revolver back into its holster.

"When hunting parties come through, and I guarantee that they will," he said gravely, "you'll be in serious trouble. Do you have any idea what they'll do to a young woman out here alone?"

Nell turned and walked over to where he'd tossed the hatchet. Fishing it out of the snow, she came back to the woodpile.

"I'm going. This is your last chance. Come with me."

Nell said nothing. She simply stared at the white notch in the wood.

Henry shook his head. Turning, he went back to his horse and pretended to be checking his gear, pulling at straps and retying the cords holding his bedroll on. He didn't look back at her, but he felt her eyes on him.

"So long," he called out.

Henry adjusted his hat, pulled up the collar of his coat, and reached down for the stirrup.

"Wait."

6

HENRY JUDGED they were making good time, in spite of the added weight on the sturdy gelding.

Nell was riding double behind him, sitting up on Henry's bearskin. She'd rolled up almost everything she needed in the canvas bedding that had once been part of a wagon canopy. She had very little, except for a battered Yellowboy rifle, a few clothes, and some dried meat that Henry added to his stock in the saddlebag. She wore the oversized wool coat, cinched at the waist with her gun belt, a wide brim hat, wool pants, boots, and mittens she'd fashioned from rabbit skin.

Henry was glad she was dressed as she was. It made sense, considering the weather and the danger of running into others. A person would have to get pretty close to her to see she was a young woman.

It was their second full day on the trail, and he and Nell had spent most of it riding along the heavily forested ridge. They'd been working their way south in order to pick up the wagon road that ran from Denver clear to Mormon country. He figured they had five more days before they reached the road. So long as the snow held off.

The smell of pine in winter was sharp and satisfying as they rode beneath the deep green canopy. The horse's hooves thudded softly on the carpet of needles.

Most of Henry's life had been spent on the trail. He'd grown up aware of the whispers and chatter and cries of the woodcock and the chipmunk and the raven. He knew when they were content and when they were restless and alarmed. The sounds and smells floated on the breezes and on the currents of the rivers. Whether he was traveling across the open plains and through the solemn gloom of the forest, he was one with the natural world. But there was also a part of him—the part he figured he inherited from his father—that liked to hear the sound of a human voice. Especially on long rides like this one.

Nell Cody wasn't much of a talker, that was for sure. Unless she had to, she didn't answer a question and didn't offer a word of conversation. So they rode along, each to their own thoughts, the silence only broken when Henry recalled a story he thought she'd enjoy. He told her about the mountains above the Bighorn River, where there were so many grizzlies that travelers needed to ride with their hunting rifles cocked and ready across their laps. And about the days when the grasslands north of the Yellowstone River were packed tight with buffalo. Once, he told her, a fellow he knew in Old Fort Alexander ran across their broad backs all the way to Canada without touching the ground once.

"You're making that up."

"Why, it's the damn truth."

Nell's amused snort said she didn't believe him.

As they were making their way around the huge trunk of a fallen tree as big as a railroad car, the dim forest light gradually brightened. In a few moments, Henry's bay carried them out into a wide-open range.

To the west, the land eventually fell away into a deep, snowy gorge. In the distance, storm clouds massed and swirled around high peaks, ominous and dark.

Something about the mountains and the snow-dusted fir trees caused Henry to hearken back to his childhood. His father didn't have much that he valued, but he'd come home from his horse-trading once with a colored print of some boys dragging pines across the snow. In the background, there was a lumber mill with mountains rising beyond it. When Henry asked why they were cutting down the saplings, his father had explained about Christmas. It was a day, he'd said, when families gathered and decorated the trees and exchanged gifts...and treated each other as special on account of the Lord coming to earth.

"You left a Bible on the grave of one of them travelers you buried."

Nell made no reply.

The army had celebrated Christmas Day with dances, reduced duties, and extra rations. There wasn't much that was religious about it.

"And a cross."

Silence.

"Why do that for him? Or was it a her?"

"Him."

"A relation of yours?"

Pulling words out of her was tougher than getting a beefsteak from a street dog.

"The man must have been a believer, I'm guessing."

"He was a pastor."

Four entire words. Downright chatty. Henry tried to keep his excitement in check.

A pastor. Henry's mother believed in the ways of the Crow people, and his father held that "religion never put food on nobody's table...except the preacher's." It wasn't until they were both gone that Henry learned about the Christian religion. The army was full of men who were believers of one type or another. But over the years, he'd also come to understand that not every man of religion was to be trusted.

Itinerant ministers were everywhere. The frontier was crawling with them. Many were probably sincere. But the West was also open territory for rascals who put on the garb of the evangelizer and spouted Scripture in order to prey on the weak-minded and the desperate. Still, he knew that "pastors" were another breed entirely. They had a church and a flock, and they cared about folks' well-being, mostly.

"So he had a church, then?"

"Yes."

"What made him give it up and come out here into the wilderness?"

Nell said nothing. She was the damnedest young woman. As tight with her talk as a miser with a grain of gold dust.

"I'll just assume you don't know." Silence. "Hell, he wasn't no pastor, at all. Probably robbed half the banks in Ohio. Rustled cattle in Missouri. Held up stage-coaches from the Badlands to—"

"No. Like I said, he had a church."

Henry waited. But she clearly didn't see any need in discussing it further.

46

All around them, knife-edged drifts framed in scattered jumbled piles of gray boulders. Some of those boulders were as large as houses. Powdery snow that covered most of the ground whipped up and stung their faces.

He looked ahead at a line of trees a few miles along the ridge.

They hadn't covered half the distance when Nell spoke up.

"Storm is coming." She pointed to the west.

Way out in the distance, one hell of a storm was barreling toward them. The gorge was already nothing more than a shadowy gray-blue blur. The mountain peaks and ridges and valleys...all gone. The advancing line of snow swallowed up everything in its path as it moved eastward.

"Yep." He'd seen it coming over the far ridge a while back, but he didn't see any point in worrying her.

"We going to get caught in it?"

"We can't outrun it." As he spoke, an icy blast of wind nearly staggered the gelding. "We'll just push ahead and hope we can find some place to wait it out."

Henry screwed his hat on tighter. Nell's head pressed against his shoulder blades.

The wall of snow continued its relentless climb, covering the open terrain. Ahead of it, the wind howled, pushing over the scattered clumps of scrub pine. The closer the storm got, the faster it came. Henry searched around them for shelter, but there was nothing.

Then, with the suddenness of a barroom brawl, the storm enveloped them in a cold white shroud, and the wind hit hard.

Day became night, with the driven snow falling so fast and heavy that Henry could barely see twenty feet ahead. Then ten. Then five.

"Can you see where you're going?" Nell shouted over the wind.

"Barely."

They forged ahead for a while until a pile of boulders loomed up ahead like some headless giant, kneeling in the snow. One huge rock slab leaned against the others, projecting outward and forming an overhang. Henry nudged the gelding toward the lee side of the shelter.

Pulling his hat down to protect his face, he relied on his horse to get them there. Every step was a struggle against the wind and the biting cold.

"C'mon, boy. You know what to do."

The sturdy gelding was a solid mountain animal. Punching holes in the snow with one hoof and then the next, he brought them under the overhang.

Henry pulled off his hat, knocked two inches of powder off the brim, and patted the bay's neck.

The protected space was high enough and wide enough to accommodate the two of them and the gelding, as well.

"We'll stop here for a while."

After the riders dismounted, Henry looked out at the blizzard. This was the kind of mountain storm that had killed a detail of soldiers out of Fort Collins back in January of '72. They didn't find what was left of the bodies until April.

He realized Nell was watching him.

"There's no telling how long this is going to last." He brushed off his coat. "A storm like this might carry on for a day or a week. We're better off waiting it out here."

"Tell me what to do."

Through the gusting snow, he saw what looked to be a fallen tree about a hundred paces off. "I'll fetch us some firewood. We might as well eat something while we wait. You tend to the horse."

She unbuckled her gun belt and laid it aside.

Henry pulled his hand axe out of a saddlebag and trudged out through the deepening snow. He needed to keep his bearings. He didn't want to gather wood and then find himself wandering off in the wrong direction.

The snow was piling up quickly. The wind was

pushing the fresh stuff into drifts, and there was a crust underneath that broke under Henry's boot with every step. At least that would help him find his way back, he thought.

As he post-holed it toward the fallen tree, he heard the muffled sound of elk trumpeting in the distance. He paused, trying to decide how close they were. An elk steak would make for a tasty supper. After a moment, he dismissed the thought. There was no way he could hunt them in this weather.

By the time he reached the fallen tree, he was warmer than he'd been all day. But that wasn't saying much.

As he began to chop away at the branches, the smell of cedar filled his senses. Even the wind couldn't whisk it away fast enough. He'd seen only a few of these trees dotting the open range land on the ridge. The wood was hard as rock, but it would make a good fire.

He was nearly finished when a dark shape flashed by. He saw it only in the corner of his eye through the falling snow. It was just a quick blur, silent as death, but he knew what it was. Then he saw another shadowy figure bounding toward the stone shelter. And another.

Wolves.

They'd been following the elk herd, but they must

have caught the scent of Henry's horse. A tired and solitary animal would be easier prey.

The wind tore the warning cry from his lips. A moment later, Nell's snow-muffled yell blended with the screams of the gelding.

Henry started to run, but his boots caught in the crust beneath the fresh snow with every step. It was a nightmare.

She shouted and cursed. The pack hadn't caught her unawares.

"Of course they hadn't," he muttered. Nell had survived a massacre and stayed alive on her own for three months. She was tough and savvy and alert.

But these wolves were hungry. They wouldn't risk a fight with a human, otherwise.

Axe in hand, Henry yanked his coat aside and went for his Colt, clearing leather in an instant.

The sound of gunfire would surely send the pack running, but he didn't get a single round off. A wolf that had been laying back hit him from the side, knocking him to the ground and sending his revolver flying into the snow.

He came up looking into the face of the wolf.

The animal was as big as any Henry had ever seen. The snow-dusted fur was gray and brown, streaked with black. The eyes were pale green. More important, the teeth and fangs were brilliant white and deadly beneath the shining red gums. And he meant business.

"Come on, *cheéte,*" Henry snarled, using the Crow word from his youth. He raised the hand axe.

The wolf lunged and backed away, looking for an opening.

Henry knew those teeth could slash though the flesh and sinews of tougher animals than himself. And those jaws had enough strength to crack a bison's rib bone.

The wolf leaped at him, a blur of gray fur.

Bracing himself, Henry batted the animal's head to the side with his left arm and swung the axe at the powerful shoulder. He felt the blade cut into the skin and muscle, and the wolf went down in the snow with a wild yelp. Another quick stroke and he lay motionless.

It took only a moment for Henry to find his Colt in the snow. When he turned, the stone shelter was momentarily visible. Nell was fighting them, and her fierce threats reached him.

There were a half-dozen wolves, and they'd formed a half-circle. She stood by the dark bay gelding, which she'd thankfully tethered to something near the back wall of the shelter. If she hadn't done it, the animal would already be off and running, blindly leading the pack until it slipped or got caught in a drift. A horse that size would feed a pack for over a week.

Nell was wielding her knife, stamping her feet, and shouting at the gray killers.

As he ran, he fired his revolver above the stone slab, and the alarmed wolves scattered in every direction.

All but one, who snatched a leather bag from the ground near Nell's feet.

The bag was smaller than a bread loaf. Nell lunged forward and got hold of it. Whatever it was, she was not about to let the wolf take it. Her hand was inches from the predator's fangs, and she wasn't letting go.

As Henry ran toward them, a tug-of-war began. The lone wolf had one end of the bag clenched in its jaws; she had the other. The beast was pulling and shaking his head, trying to wrest it from Nell's grip. She was no less determined, hanging on and stabbing at the animal with her knife.

Henry couldn't get a clean shot, so he fired the pistol into the air again.

As the shot rang out, the wolf released the prize and darted off. Nell fell backward, and the bag flew from her hand, landing in the snow.

7

NELL'S BODY WAS SHAKING, and she couldn't get it to stop. Her breaths were coming short. A flush of heat started in her face and washed down through her shoulders and back. Her heart was pounding in her chest and in her ears.

She could have been torn apart by that pack of killers. She was close enough to the wolf to smell his breath. She stared into the snow-filled gloom in the direction they'd gone.

Henry moved, and she jumped to her feet. Smoke trailed from the gun in his hand. He was a wall of protection against the predators.

In his sermons, her father spoke of the heroes in the Bible. In Nell's mind, Henry Jordan was also a hero.

Strong and wise and chivalrous, in his own rough-hewn frontier way.

Since they'd been traveling together, Nell had been thinking how fortunate she was that he showed up at the cabin door. She was relieved she hadn't killed him right off. Grateful that he'd been convincing enough about the dangers she'd be facing alone to get on the road with him. Before he came, she didn't have any choice but to stay in that cabin. But now she doubted that she could have survived the winter in the mountains. And even if, by some miracle, she did survive, the spring didn't offer the promise of anyone trustworthy passing through.

All the threats he spoke of were real. She'd witnessed firsthand the cruelty that men were capable of. And now this. These wolves meant to have them for their supper.

Even as the thought passed through her mind, the howls of the pack could be heard over the wind and snow.

"Are they coming back?"

"No." His reply was curt. "They're gathering. Licking their wounds. They won't come back."

"Good."

Henry turned toward her, and she saw anger blazing in his eyes.

"You almost got yourself killed. If he'd gone for your throat instead of *this*..." He kicked at the leather bag. "You tell me, is whatever you've got in here worth losing your life for?"

They both looked down. The bag had opened, and three bundles of bank notes, neatly tied with string, had spilled out. The breeze riffled the ends of the bills.

Nell crouched down and began stuffing the money back inside.

"What's this?"

"Bank notes."

"Your folks' money?"

Before they'd set out from the cabin, her immediate reaction would have been to warn him off. Packing her meager belongings, she'd been careful to hide the money in her satchel. But he'd seen it now. There was no sense in keeping the secret from him. Besides, Henry had saved her life.

"No. This isn't mine. It belongs to the people of Youngblood Creek, where our wagons were headed. That's why I still have to go there. It's my responsibility to deliver this money to them."

"That's a lot to ask of someone your age."

"Who else is left? I'm the only one who survived. And my father..." Nell's voice hitched as the image of him clutching his bloody chest came back to her.

She'd been angry at him the night of the attack. She'd been upset with him from the moment they left Boulder. Since then, she'd had plenty of time to think through her actions and the way she'd spoken to him. If she could take all of it back, she would. But she couldn't. He was gone. But a promise was a promise. She couldn't give him her word when he was alive, but she'd honor his wish now...and with every last ounce of strength left in her.

"My father was entrusted with it. And he gave me the money—asked me to deliver it—right before he died."

"What's the money for?"

She took a deep breath. "It's for building a church and later, a school."

Trusting him lifted a weight off her shoulders. A feeling of relief flowed through her. She was no longer alone.

The wind and snow howled around them, and Nell shivered.

"We'll freeze, standing around here." Henry holstered his pistol. "Let's get a fire going. You can tell me more later."

Nell stuffed the bag under her bedroll.

Henry started to go after the wood, but hesitated and glanced over his shoulder. "Will you be safe enough here?"

Nell stood up and strapped on her Colt. She'd taken it off when she began tending to the horse. "I'll be fine."

The howls of the wolves again cut through the sound of the storm. She stared in the direction they were coming from.

"Why are they still around?"

Henry gestured toward the fallen tree. "Because one of them is lying dead over there. They don't know it yet. They're hoping he'll find his way to them."

"Are *you* all right? You didn't get hurt?"

"I'm just fine. You have any trouble, use that iron." Pulling his hat on tighter, Henry headed back out into the storm to get the wood.

Nell watched him go. The man's long, brown hair whipped around his broad shoulders. Like Samson. He was just a blur through the falling snow when he stopped by a dark form lying on the ground. The wolf he'd killed. He picked up his hand axe and continued on until he faded from her view.

The storm had hit them fast and hard. They were high in the mountains. What they were facing was far harsher than what she'd faced at the cabin or in Boulder. They were fortunate that Henry had found this shelter. Above her head, a stone slab projected a good fifteen feet beyond the upright boulder and served as a roof. Smaller rocks jutted out of the frozen ground on either side, linked by drifts to form low walls.

The wind shifted out of the north for a moment, showering Nell with wisps of snow. She moved their things close to the rock, where they'd be protected. The horse pawed the ground, obviously happy to be under cover and safe from the predators.

With a fire, she judged, this was as good a place as a person could expect, here on the open range.

Nell again gazed out in the direction the wolves had gone. After the massacre, she'd thought she was prepared for anything that the wilderness threw at her. But she was wrong. For all those months, she never had to face a wolf or a bear. She never had to kill an animal larger than a rabbit or a racoon.

According to Henry, they still had a long way to go before they reached the wagon road and from there to Denver. But that wasn't her destination. She broke out in a sweat trying to think how she was going to find her way to Youngblood Creek.

Nell cast a glance toward Henry. No sign of him. Worry pitted in her stomach. What if some other kind of beast went after him out in the open?

Then, as if he knew she was wishing him back, his form emerged from the storm. With wood piled high in his arms, Henry trudged directly to the shelter.

"Good. I was getting ready to come after you."

The look he sent her was one of amusement.

A few moments later, they had a fire going.

The sunless day was quickly giving way to night, but the storm continued unabated. The snow was swirling on the gusts of wind, sparkling in the light from the flames.

Henry squatted by the fire, warming his hands. "You wanna tell me about this money and Youngblood Creek?"

Nell's mind went back to the beginning of summer, when her father first told her about their upcoming adventure. An opportunity awaited them in the new community in the mountains, a hundred miles to the west of Boulder. The folks already there were eager to build a church. He'd have a devoted flock. The frontier town was a much better place for them to be living than in the bustle and grime of the city.

She thought he'd lost his mind. John Cody had a church and a sizable congregation. They had a home. She argued with him, trying to get him to see that there was no reason for them to go. No reason to leave behind what they had. But he wouldn't listen. He'd made up his mind. His plans were already in the works.

Nell realized that she wasn't sharing any of that out loud when Henry tossed another piece of wood onto the fire. Sparks rose up on the smoke, only to be whisked away by the wind.

"Chatterbox that you are, I'm thinking that it might be best if I ask some questions to get the cart moving."

"Very well. Ask away."

"The pastor you buried back there. The one with the cross and the Bible marking his grave."

"My father, John Cody."

Henry paused. "I'm sorry. I figured."

With the snow still falling hard and the wind whistling across the blackness of the open range, Nell watched the flames cast shadows on the stone wall of their shelter.

After finding the cabin, she'd had to take two separate trips back to the wagons to bury the bodies. The first time, she'd followed the smoke. Little tongues of fire still flickered from glowing embers in the charred remains, and the acrid smell hung like a cloud over their camp. The work of burying the dead was exhausting and heart-wrenching. Covering her father's body was the saddest and the hardest thing she'd ever done in her life. With each stone she added to the pile, another memory flooded back. After they were buried, she visited the site often to pay her respects.

"And your mother? Was she with you? Or any other kin?"

She stared at a patch of glistening snow that was melting a few feet from the fire. Gravel and rock and last year's dead grass lay exposed. "No. I lost her three years ago. The two of us were all that was left."

Her father sold their house before they left Boulder. Since then, she had recurring dreams of hearing her mother's voice. But even though she seemed to be close by, Nell couldn't find her.

"How many people were in your party?"

"Fourteen, including our guide."

"Same destination?"

"Yes, we were all going to Youngblood Creek."

"And everybody but you was killed?"

"No. Bart Kelly, the man we'd hired to guide us, didn't die. He was in on it."

Nell heard him curse under his breath. Henry had said he'd heard of such villainy before.

"He had his men waiting to ambush you on the road?"

"Yes."

"You want to tell me about it?"

She did. She needed to. For months now, she'd been brimming with anger at the crime.

Once Nell started, the words all came free like puffs of thistledown. She told him how the underhanded attack came in the middle of the night while everyone was sleeping. How the travelers had tried to fight but had little chance of defending themselves. How the massacre was over in just a few minutes. Men, women, and children...all cut down. She also told him of her father's death before she escaped into the forest.

"How many bushwhackers came at you?"

"Four. Plus Kelly. One of them was killed." She didn't see any point in telling him that she did the killing. She felt no guilt. She'd do it again. Of all the nightmares that had been haunting her since the night of the attack, killing that man hadn't been part of them. "They meant to murder us all."

The two sat in silence for a while. Henry stared into the fire, glancing up at her from time to time.

"That's a terrible thing you lived through, Nell. I've lived out here my whole life. Seen some horrible things done to people. Seems the worst happens when men get together and form a pack...like Kelly and them four."

"Like the wolves that came for us."

"Except them wolves were only trying to feed themselves. Nothing cruel in that. These fellas, however, are the lowest of the low. Calling them mangy dogs is an insult to mangy dogs. Every damn one of them deserves to die. And maybe their evildoing will catch up to them one day. It don't always happen, but we can always hope."

They let that thought sit for a few minutes.

"So you still plan on getting that money to Youngblood Creek." He didn't say it as a question.

"Yes. They're waiting for it. My father's dying wish was for me to deliver it to them." She decided he should know all of it. "There's $6000 in that bag."

Henry looked up at her. Nell knew from going through his saddlebags that the sum she carried was far more than he had.

His brow furrowed. "You think this Bart Kelly knew your father had that much money?"

"I think he did." Nell was too angry to be part of the planning. She had no idea how the money was raised or how many people were involved. "The more I've thought about it since, the more I think Kelly took the job because of it."

"I wouldn't be surprised. And I'll bet he's done this before."

She agreed. "The attack was perfectly planned. Right down to the place where we camped for the night."

"Yep. And far enough away from Boulder that they could do it again to another group of folks going west."

"This money—if you'll help me get to Youngblood Creek—I'm sure those people will pay you. Give you a reward."

Henry looked out into the darkness for a moment. He'd said enough times that he wanted to get to Denver as soon as possible. His partner was waiting for him.

"You know anyone, any families or folks you could stay with?"

She'd lost both parents. She had no siblings. The only relations she had were an aunt and uncle back East that she'd never met. She was all alone.

"No one. But they invited my father to come and bring me along. His name might mean something, especially if I bring their money. I have to believe they'll let me stay."

"What'll you do?"

"I've been thinking about that. I'm very good with reading, arithmetic, science. You name it, I was taught it. My parents were big on education. My plan was to teach school if I were to stay in Boulder. I can do the same thing in Youngblood Creek."

"You're so young."

"Not on the frontier."

Henry stared into the fire, a frown creasing his forehead.

"And if I take you to Denver?"

"I'll find someone there to take me on the next leg of my journey. I told you, I have a job to do and I have a better chance at Youngblood Creek than in Denver."

In the distance, the wolves began to howl again, their cries muffled by the blowing snow. The sounds were coming from farther away, but the killers were still out there.

He shook his head and cursed under his breath.

"All right. I'll take you to Youngblood Creek. Not for no reward, but for you."

8

A DUSKY GLOOM had descended by the time Henry and Nell rode into the grimy, foul-smelling port town perched on the bend of the river. Brown liquid filled knee-deep ruts in the freezing mud of the road. The smoke from a hundred fires was so dense, it cut off the darkening sky like a lid clamped down tight on a pot.

Portistown was a shit hole, to be sure. Built as a trading post by Charlie Portis before the war, the place still served as a final outpost for mountain men and for miners betting their lives on finding gold or silver in the wilds of the high country. Most didn't collect on that bet. Some did manage to survive and find something. And if they did, they found that Portis and his descendants were more than willing to supply them with all the entertainments that would separate them from their money.

Henry had known more than one fellow who'd woken up, broke and brandy sick, far downriver on one of the flat-bottomed riverboats.

It was a necessary stop, but Henry wasn't approaching the place blind. They'd been traveling steadily for four days since the storm blew itself out and they could ride again. Deep snow had slowed them down and made the trip more arduous.

They were here to get Nell a mount of her own. The gelding was tired. She was tired. Henry was tired. A fresh horse for her and a good night's sleep for the two of them would do them all a world of good.

THAT IS, if they could find a decent place to bed down. At first glance, Henry had his doubts. But it was only for one night.

In making the decision to change directions and go west to Youngblood Creek, Henry had added more than a week to his trip. He hoped his partner would still be waiting for him in Denver when he arrived.

Henry eyed the town, looking it over as they rode through. Soot covered three brothels and a dozen saloons, gambling establishments and brandy holes. A number of buildings along the road were nothing more than charred wood and ash. Apparently, no one had thought to clear the debris away. They passed the famous trading depot, a provisions store, and a livery barn. A pair of warehouses guarded a wooden wharf, where three boats were locked in by brown ice. The river wasn't frozen all the way across. A narrow passage of water was visible in the middle.

In front of one of the larger saloons—from which the energetic but horribly off-key sawing on a fiddle could be heard—a crowd of drunken miners and trappers and rivermen were jostling each other for better views as they cheered on a knife fight between two mud-covered combatants. The moving line of spectators shouted and cursed at the two fighters, egging them on as wagers on the outcome were being exchanged on the periphery.

Winter may have shut down the river trade, but it didn't seem to hurt other business in the town, at all. Henry already regretted bringing Nell here.

He gave the crowd a wide berth. While he searched for a decent hotel, they happened to pass a sheriff's office with a shuttered window and a closed door. The only place where business was slow. Someone probably shot the sheriff, he thought.

As he nudged the gelding along the road, Henry

kept his eye on the wooden walkway that ran along the fronts of the buildings. Rough-looking loiterers were sitting on barrels and crates and leaning against the unpainted siding.

Henry made an obvious point of unfastening the thong over the Colt and loosening the six-gun in its holster when he noticed every one of the idlers was paying special attention to Nell.

Down near the wharf, gunshots rang out as a throng of men, whooping wildly, spilled out of a gambling house. In the center, a trapper was staggering and brandishing a smoking revolver. The drunken reveler fired several more shots in the air, taking out an upper window across the way and nearly killing an onlooker.

Henry reined in his horse at a hotel where a boy with a severely bowed back was lighting torches in front. The sign above the door proclaimed it was THE RIVERSIDE'S FINEST ESTABLISHMENT, but from what he'd seen of the town, that wasn't much of a claim.

The hotel was a three-story affair with a pair of windows facing the street on each floor. Discarded barrels and crates and trash were piled up in an alleyway next to the building.

Without climbing down from his saddle, Henry looked through a grimy window. Inside, it was fairly crowded, with men drinking and playing faro. The only woman in evidence was standing behind a counter. A board with two rows of nails for keys was on the wall behind her.

"Got two rooms?" he asked the hunchbacked employee.

The young fellow studied them for a moment. "Think we do." He cast a meaningful glance at Nell. "I know we got *one*."

"Need *two* rooms," Henry said curtly.

"Have to ask my ma."

"We'll wait."

The son of the hotel proprietor went in.

Henry turned his head to speak to Nell. "*If* we go in here, don't look at nobody. And let me do the talking."

He knew he didn't need to say any more. She was smart to know that a young woman in a rough frontier town like this brought the risk of trouble.

The son came out, jerking a thumb back at the hotel entrance. "She says yes."

"Watch my horse for a few minutes."

Henry tossed two bits at him as Nell climbed down. Carrying the saddlebags and her satchel and their rifles, they climbed the wooden steps to the walkway.

The hotel saloon was a shabby, smoky, dismal place. The manager was staring at them from the high counter straight through at the back. To her left, a set of stairs led to the upper floors.

Henry had seen a hundred places like this over the years. A scarred wooden counter ran along the right side of the room. A few men were leaning against it, drinking and smoking. A row of tables lined the left wall. The room grew silent as soon as they entered.

Henry ran a hard gaze over the crowd and then looked at the barman—a balding, scar-faced bruiser chewing on the stub of a cigar and wearing a shiny black vest over a collarless black shirt. The man stood with his thumbs tucked into a filthy apron.

The proprietor watched them approach. She was tight-lipped and hardly hospitable as Henry paid for the rooms and took the keys and two candles that she slid across the counter.

"Top of the stairs. Second floor. The two rooms in the front," she snapped. "Them is feather beds and clean sheets. So no sleeping in 'em with your boots on. You can light your candles from the one in the hallway."

He tapped one of the keys on the counter, drawing the woman's cool gaze.

"Does your barman handle any trouble down here?"

"Him and me both, mister." She reached down and produced a short-barreled Greener from behind the counter.

Turning away, Henry ran his eyes over the crowd. The card-playing and drinking and talking had gradually begun again.

"Stay close," he said to Nell.

At the top of the stairs, a window opened out onto the back of the building, providing the only light, other than a single candle that flickered on the wall halfway down the passage.

Five doors opened off either side of the central hallway. They were all closed, and he heard no sounds coming from any of them. He glanced out the window into a muddy, snow-edged yard where two kitchen workers sat on crates beneath a flaring torch, smoking and plucking geese.

Leading Nell to the two doors that faced them at the end, Henry tested the lock on one and then opened it as she lit her candle in the hallway.

The room was empty and cold as a turtle's tit, and it offered roughly the same level of comfort as his army barracks in Wyoming. A wardrobe beside the door, a chair, a bed, and a washstand. With one hand on his iron, he pulled open the wardrobe. Empty. The muffled sounds of the men downstairs drifted up through the floorboards.

Henry crossed the room and looked out the window. It was nearly dark, but the road and the wooden sidewalk was still busy with traffic. The hotel worker was standing by Henry's horse and staring at a string of packhorses passing by, laden with furs and hides. The hunter leading them rode with his rifle laid across his lap. Henry pulled the cotton curtains closed.

He pushed down on the mattress. "A molting chicken must've walked across a heap of straw somewhere. Because that's as close to being a feather bed as this ever came."

She came in. "It's fine. The room's clean."

"You'll be all right in here." He handed her the key.

She fitted her candle into a holder and glanced under the bed. Dropping her satchel on the bare wood floor, she pushed the curtain aside and looked out.

Henry started for the door, where he stopped. "I got to take the horse down to the livery. Hopefully, they'll have something decent for you to ride."

Nell leaned her rifle against the wall by the bed. She kept her hat and coat and gun belt on.

"I don't have to tell you to lock this door. I'll be back as quick as I can."

"I'll be fine."

"I'll bring something to eat." Henry gestured toward the rifle. "And don't hesitate to shoot any varmint that tries to come in here. Except me."

"Except you," she said with a half-smile.

As Henry went into the hallway, he heard the key turn in Nell's door. Dropping his rifle and saddlebags in the other room, he locked up and went back down the stairs.

A moment later, as he went past the bar and out the front door, he didn't notice four men sitting at a table in the corner, talking in low tones and watching him go.

9

NELL LISTENED to the sound of Henry's boots moving down the hallway.

Rustic. That was the word her father would have used to describe the room. It smelled of tobacco and spilt liquor and men's sweat. The walls were unvarnished wood, darkened over the years. The floor was worn and marked by scores of boots. The wardrobe was small, and it leaned to one side. The straight chair wobbled when she put her hand on it, and the mismatched bowl and ewer on the washstand were both covered with a spiderweb of cracks. A battered spittoon that she didn't plan on using sat in the corner.

Still, as rough and musty and cold as it was, the room and the bed offered more comfort than the cabin where she'd spent the last three months. Practically luxurious, compared to the hard ground she'd been sleeping on since starting on this journey with Henry.

The sound of men's voices from the saloon downstairs reached Nell. Wariness ran through her. The relative safety of the room perched on one side of the scale, the danger of drunken men perched on the other.

Crossing to the door, she tried the knob. It was locked, but she had a feeling the only person it would keep out was an honest man.

Tossing her hat onto the chair, she put her shoulder to the side of the wardrobe. It was fairly heavy, but Nell managed to slide it in front of the door. She stood back and admired her handiwork, deciding that Henry would approve.

She crossed the room, drew back the curtains, and opened the casement window. The air outside was cold and smoky, but she took a deep breath. A cloud formed as she let it escape slowly from her lungs.

Below her, Henry was on the sidewalk, speaking with the bow-backed boy. The last time she'd seen him from this angle, she almost shot him. The young fellow gestured down the road. Henry pulled on his gloves and swung up easily into the saddle.

For a moment, her eyes lingered on the man who'd taken her quest as his own.

Nell knew she looked young for her age. But at

fifteen, she'd had a number of crushes on boys back in Boulder. As soon as they found out her father was a pastor, though, they ran for the hills.

Henry was so different from all those boys. He was honorable. There were plenty of instances where he'd proven that to her since they'd met.

He'd mentioned that he was twenty-six. That made him almost eleven years older than her. Not so much. Her parents had a larger age difference between them.

Henry was tall, much taller even than her father. His eyes were brown, his shoulders wide. Riding behind him, she'd had ample opportunity to feel the strength of his muscles through the leather coat, to see the hints of red in his long hair as it curled at his shoulders. He had a sense of humor. And he was sensitive. He cared about her opinion. That was a lot to say for any man.

What she thought of him was a daydream. Henry had not shown an ounce of interest in her as a woman. Honorable. Honorable. Honorable. But repeating the obvious didn't stop Nell from making comparisons to another man that she respected.

As close as she'd been to her father, John Cody saw his ministry as his one true calling. That was true when Nell's mother was alive. And nothing changed after she passed. Everything else came in a distant second. Nell knew he loved her, in his own way. But to him, she was more of a duty to discharge. A responsibility left to him by his wife, a girl to be raised correctly and kept safe.

Nell didn't think her father ever realized that she was growing up. When they pulled up stakes and headed for Youngblood Creek, not once did he ask her opinion about anything. That was just his way. All her complaining fell on deaf ears.

Since the attack on the wagons, however, everything had changed. She had to make all the decisions, learn how to survive. She'd even killed a man. There was no one else to help her, to protect her. She'd matured years in those three months. Maybe she was still a child back in Boulder, but no more. She was an adult.

Nell loved her father, but he was gone now. She was on her own.

Below her, as Henry nudged the dark bay toward the livery, two men stepped out of the hotel saloon. They stared at his back, and then one gestured for his partner to follow Henry on the other side of the road.

"What in the blazes?"

She recalled the army pay she'd seen among Henry's things and wondered if that's what they were after. She glanced over at her satchel. He'd brought his saddlebag in. He must have left it in his room.

The men were moving quickly. Almost immediately, she lost sight of the fellow on this side. But as the other crossed the muddy road, she saw him unfasten the thong holding his revolver. He never took his eyes off of Henry.

"You vile, lowdown weasels. You're up to no good."

Nell's initial thought was that she needed to warn him. She glanced at the door she'd blocked. If she moved the wardrobe out of the way, she'd still need to go through the saloon downstairs. She looked out the window. It was about an eight-foot drop to the wooden sidewalk. A bit high, but not terrible.

Even though it was growing dark, the road and the sidewalks were filled with people. They wouldn't dare do him harm with so many folks looking on. At least, she hoped they wouldn't.

The men following Henry disappeared among a large throng in front of a saloon up the road.

She gripped the gun at her hip. If she went after them right now, what could she do that he couldn't do for himself? Henry had been a soldier. He was as comfortable in the wilderness as anyone she'd ever met. He was always on the alert for danger. He could protect himself, she hoped.

Before the thought could settle, Nell heard people on the steps down the hall. She spun around and stared at the door. It sounded like an army coming up. The boots on the stair treads were heavy.

"Keep an eye open. She *ain't* getting away."

She. Nell froze. Were they looking for her?

A door down the hallway creaked open.

"Not here."

"Try the next one."

"It's locked."

"Open the damn thing."

Her heart jumped at the sound of wood cracking as they forced a door.

"Nothing."

They were checking rooms. They'd waited until Henry left, and the woman downstairs had let them come up.

Another lock broke. A door opened and then shut.

"Get the next one."

Nell scanned the room quickly. There was nowhere to hide.

She glanced at the rifle leaning against the wall. She'd gotten good at shooting with it at the cabin, but she wasn't fast enough when it came to cocking the lever between shots. It would be useless to try and fight more than one person with it.

She heard another door down the hall forced open.

Staring at the wardrobe, Nell realized, too late, that the piece of furniture wouldn't be enough to keep them out. She needed something bigger, stronger.

The bed! No, it was too heavy for her to move quickly.

How many more rooms before they reached hers? She hadn't counted them. But they were getting closer.

Nell pushed back at the panic edging into her brain.

The next door to hers banged open. "Nope."

Heavy footsteps approached, and Nell felt her heart drop like a cold stone into her stomach.

A low growl. "This it?"

"Gotta be. Or that one."

"What about the third floor?"

"I told you I heard the woman say, *second* floor."

Nell backed against the wall by the window, staring at the door.

"She was carrying a rifle...and wearing a rod."

There was no doubt about it. They *were* looking for her.

"Open it."

"Call her out. She might come out on her own."

"You afraid of a girl, all of a sudden?"

"I ain't afraid of nothing," the man growled back.

"Then let's go."

The wardrobe didn't cover the door completely, and Nell could see the knob being turned. They were testing the lock. She knew what was coming next.

She put her hand on the grip of her Colt.

That door was thin, like all the others. It wouldn't hold them. And that wardrobe would barely slow them down at all.

Should she stand and fight? She didn't actually know how many men were out there. How many could she hit before she was killed?

"You're *sure* she's the one?"

Annoyance darkened the responding snarl. "It's her. It's Cody's daughter. Now open the damn door."

Bart Kelly. It had to be him. The surly frontiersman who led her father and the others to slaughter. The devil who pretended to care about getting the wagon train safely to Youngblood Creek. The fiend who arranged for his murderous friends to lie in wait and kill everyone.

Cody's daughter. Somehow, he'd seen her and recognized her. He must have been downstairs when they came in, Nell thought.

Then, another thought made her blood run cold. The two men who went after Henry were part of his gang. The same monsters who'd ambushed the wagons.

She jumped at the heavy thump of a shoulder hitting the door, accompanied by an exerted grunt.

"You think she still has it?"

"It don't matter a damn," Kelly snapped. "She knows me. Probably knows you too. Ain't that reason enough?"

It wasn't just the money. He wanted her, and they wanted her *dead*.

Maybe they would kill her. But maybe she could put a bullet in Kelly's chest first. Images of dead bodies scattered throughout their camp came back to her. She could avenge her father's murder. Avenge all of their murders.

Nell wanted to kill Bart Kelly, but she had something more important that she needed to do. The promise she'd made to her father. Getting revenge had to take second place to fulfilling his dying wish.

She grabbed her satchel.

A second thump was accompanied by the *crack* of breaking wood as the door splintered around the lock. It popped open an inch, moving the piece of furniture with it. Another shove from the outside, and the wardrobe moved two more inches.

"Push the damn thing open."

She looked out the window. There would be no climbing down. She'd have to jump.

Another shove succeeded in pushing the wardrobe back enough for Kelly's head to fit through.

Their gazes locked for only an instant. Then, the barrel of his revolver appeared.

Turning, Nell leaped out the window.

10

HENRY DISMOUNTED by the open barn doors of the livery stable and ran his hand over the gelding's neck. "You done real good, fella. I do believe there's something extra coming your way."

Located at the far end of town from the river, the livery stable offered no surprises to Henry. To the right of the barn, a score of wagons and carts in a wide range of disrepair filled a snowy and muddy yard. A large, fenced corral ran up a hill before disappearing into the smoky darkness. More than a dozen horses and mules gathered close to the barn, watching him attentively.

Across the way, a squeeze-box started up in a saloon that was hemmed in by a pair of whorehouses. As soon as the music started, a chorus of men immediately joined in. It was a popular Stephen Foster song. There were quite a few men milling about the doors of the brandy hole and the brothels, and it was even more boisterous now than when he and Nell had ridden in.

Portistown was one place he wouldn't be visiting again anytime soon. Trouble followed Henry. It'd been that way his whole life. Having the sense to watch for it, he noticed the solitary figure clomp along the sidewalk and stop in the shadows next to the saloon's window. The man leaned against the wall, but he was looking straight at the livery.

At the same time, a drifter ambled by the gate to the stable yard and paused to put one boot up on the fence. He had his wool coat open where he could get at the brace of Winchesters he wore cross-holstered. The drifter was a gun hawk, without a doubt.

Henry decided that both of these coyotes bore watching.

Loosening his Colt in the holster, he led the dark bay inside, where the stableman was lighting a lantern.

He nodded to Henry and limped over. "Evening. Whaddya need?"

Henry handed him the reins of the bay. "I need you to take good care of this fella. He could use some extra oats and a good brushing."

"How long you staying?"

"Just tonight." The livery was no different from a

hundred others he'd seen in a hundred frontier towns. On the left, a door opened into a tiny office, where another lit lamp sat on a table. An unmade cot stood against the wall. A dozen stalls lined the back wall, and the hay loft appeared to be well-stocked for the winter. To the left, two large feed bins were visible beyond a tack room. "Got a stall for him?"

"Yep. Cost ya."

"He deserves it. We been on the trail for a few weeks now, and he's been tough as a one-eyed trooper."

"Uh-huh."

"And I need to buy a good horse, if you got something worth my money. And a saddle."

The livery man brightened up. "Sure. Got a good-looking gray that I just bought off a cowboy who needed cash. Damn good-looking animal, in fact."

"Nothing too big or too frisky. The rider don't have a helluva lot of experience in the saddle."

As soon as the words were out, he decided they were a mistake. He had no idea what kind of rider Nell was. She was certainly better at surviving in the wilderness than any young white person of her age, boy or girl.

"Aside from the gray, got a couple of mounts that might suit ya. Matter of fact, got one mare as docile as a newborn lamb and surefooted as a mule. Give me a minute. I'll bring her in."

"Let me see the gray too."

Before the stableman could lead the gelding away, a noise from the yard caused Henry to spin around, his hand on his iron.

A horse and rider ambled calmly into the yard, stopping just outside of the glow of the lantern.

Henry saw that the two fellows who'd caught his eye had disappeared.

The newcomer wore a cloak of buffalo skin over a black wool coat. His wide brim hat made it impossible to read his face, but Henry knew the sharp eyes were assessing him. He was lean and tough-looking.

The stableman knew him. "Hullo, Marshal."

The lawman lifted his chin a whisker, never taking his eyes off of Henry. "Abe."

Henry relaxed the grip on his pistol.

"Didn't expect to see you back here so soon."

"The pass north of here was snowed in." He motioned to Henry's gelding. "Hope you ain't planning on going that way, mister."

Henry shook his head. "Nope. Heading a few days west of here."

The marshal climbed down, stretched, and shrugged out of the buffalo cloak, which he threw over the saddle. He wore a pair of Colt Peacemakers low on his hips. A bona fide pistoleer. Henry had a good idea that he could handle himself in a tight spot.

The lawman was a few inches shorter than him, but his lean frame was straight. He wore a graying mustache, and it trailed down the sides of a mouth. He struck Henry as a sort who didn't smile much.

"Where to...west of here?"

Deciding that the lawman was just being cordial, he shrugged. "A place called Youngblood Creek. You know it?"

"Sure do. Get up there pretty regular."

"Regular?" Henry frowned. "For trouble?"

"Hell, no," the marshal scoffed. "Fine folks up there. Building something good. Want to keep it that way."

Just then, a quarrel broke out on the sidewalk in front of the saloon across the road. The lawman watched it for a moment, but the altercation didn't escalate. The scufflers went off in separate directions.

Henry gestured toward them. "I'd think a town like this could use a sheriff...regular."

"And you'd be right." He tossed the reins to the stableman, who led the horses away. "This place can't keep one. If they ain't shot in the back, they hightail out of here quick enough. Nice and quiet this time of year, but when the ice breaks up, it can look like hell is empty and all the devils is here."

As if on cue, a dozen shots rang out at the far end of town.

Henry chuckled. "Nice and quiet."

The marshal's mustache pulled upward on one side. "Shoulda been here in the week after statehood was announced. Why, it was a damn miracle only three men was killed, what with all the carousing and shooting and general mayhem."

Henry peered into the darkness of the barn. He didn't want to leave Nell alone too long.

"The name's Elliot Wright."

"Jordan. Henry Jordan."

"Just out of the army?"

"How could you tell?"

"A man's got a look to him." Wright shrugged. "But maybe I been a marshal too long."

"Well, you're right. Just out."

The marshal didn't seem to be in any hurry to move along. "What takes you to Youngblood Creek?"

He thought about how much to tell the fellow. He'd known plenty of lawmen who he wouldn't trust as far as he could spit, but this fellow seemed all right.

"Found a young woman, Nell Cody, up in the mountains. She was going there with her father, a minister. They were part of a wagon train that got ambushed three months ago."

The marshal's eyes narrowed. "Ambushed by who?"

"It was a set-up. The guide they hired in Boulder had four bushwhackers waiting."

"I didn't hear nothing about it."

"'Cuz nobody was left alive to do the telling...except the one I found."

Wright planted a gloved fist into the palm of his other hand. "Got a name to this guide?"

"Bart Kelly."

The marshal shook his head. "Never heard of him."

Henry shrugged. "Him and the rest of his gang could be down in Mexico by now, enjoying the good life."

"Maybe. But I wanna make sure. I don't particularly care for filthy curs like that operating in my territory. Maybe I should talk to this young woman, if you don't..."

Nell's voice came from the darkness outside the stable doors, stopping the marshal mid-sentence.

"Drop your gun, or I'll kill you where you stand."

11

———————

HENRY CLEARED LEATHER.

Though Nell was no more than a dozen paces away, he couldn't see her. He didn't know who she was holding a gun on, but she wouldn't have left the hotel unless trouble came knocking.

"Henry, they found me," she called out. "Bart Kelly and his gang. I've got one of them dead in my sights here."

Before he could move, two of the horses in the stalls behind him whinnied nervously. As he turned away from the barn door, a gunshot lit the darkness, and lead nicked the shoulder of his elkskin coat. He dove toward the livery office.

Another shot rang out, and the marshal spun to the ground.

The same low-down sidewinder had fired both shots. Right now, Henry and the lawman were between him and the barn door, where Nell held the other one at gunpoint. He recalled the two men who were watching him before Elliot Wright arrived. They had to be the same ones.

"Nell, you all right?" Henry shouted, seeing the lawman roll toward cover.

"I've got a gun pointed at this one, but there's more coming."

"How many, altogether?"

"Four maybe," she called out. "But I'm not sure."

"If that one even breathes, *shoot* the bastard." He turned to the marshal, who was attempting to stand. The man's right arm hung limp at his side. "How about you?"

"I'll live." The lawman drew with his left. "Worry about her."

Henry hated the fact that she was out there alone, but this blackguard by the stalls had him pinned down.

The gunman fired twice from the rear of the barn. One slug buried itself in the wall of the livery office.

Before Henry could move, shots erupted outside. They came from the road beyond the livery yard, and lead thudded into wall of the barn like a drum roll. It was too much to hope that some good Samaritan was coming to help. He figured the rest of Kelly's men had arrived.

Nell returned fire, and an instant later a gunslick darted across the barn threshold, running hard for the tack room. Fanning his six-gun, he sprayed bullets before he disappeared through the open door.

"Nell?" Henry shouted.

"He got away from me."

"I'm coming for you."

"Don't. I'm good."

He was here because of Nell. He'd promised to get her to Youngblood Creek, and he'd damn well do it. The trouble was that the dog now in the tack room had the barn door covered, and the shooter in the rear of the stable would gun him down if he tried to make a run anyway.

More rounds exchanged outside. She didn't have enough bullets in her pistol to hold them off.

"Nell, I need you to get clear of the door."

"I'm...I'm going."

"*Now!*"

The gunman in the shadowy recesses of the livery fired again, and Henry aimed at the muzzle flash. His bullet found its target, for the dark shape of a man fell with a loud grunt against a stall before dropping in a heap.

"One down," he muttered. He turned his attention back to the yard. "Nell?"

No answer. No sound or movement outside, at all. The music from the saloon had stopped when the shooting started.

"She cleared out," the marshal whispered across the space. "Went to the left."

Henry reloaded quickly before glancing at the entry to the tack room. Immediately, the shooter threw lead at him.

Henry fired back, burying bullets in the doorway of the tack room and raising splinters only inches from the bushwhacker's face. The cur retreated.

Suddenly, shots rang out from a stall on the barn's back wall. A third gunman had gotten himself where he could catch the lawman in a crossfire. If the marshal moved from behind the post, the gun hawk in the tack room would plug him. If he stayed where he was, the newcomer would surely cut him down.

Henry's Colt spit fire at the tack room and then at the shooter in the stall, trying to keep them busy while the marshal got himself to safety.

But Elliot Wright showed no interest in moving. With his back to the post, he waited calmly for the new shooter to move. A hat appeared above the wall of the stall. That was all the lawman needed. His Peacemaker cracked, the hat flew off, and another killer lit out on the road to eternity.

Clouds of thick gun smoke swirled around the lantern and slowly rose into the barn rafters.

The man in the tack room must have realized that he was alone. "Listen, I don't have no beef with you fellas. Let's make a deal."

"You ain't exactly coming at this from strength, you sack of shit." The marshal's voice was hard. "The only deal is this, you come out with your hands in the air and maybe I'll let you live."

"That ain't right," the killer whined. "I ain't done nothing to you."

"You and this no-good pack you run with have fired upon a US Marshal."

The gun hawk was done bargaining. He exploded out of the tack room like his ass was on fire. With pistols in both hands, he ran sideways for the barn door, blasting at both Henry and Wright as he went.

But Henry was not about to let him get any closer to Nell. His bullet caught the man square in the chest at the same moment the marshal's slug hit him in the side. He took one more step and then tumbled to the ground, his revolvers dropping into the dirt.

Henry was out of the office in a flash and headed for the barn door. Before he could reach it, another voice came from the back of the stable. "Looking for this one?"

He whirled to see a mountain man wearing fringed leather standing behind Nell. He was half-hidden behind a post. The trail guide was holding a gun to her temple and clutching the collar of her coat with the other hand.

"Don't hurt her," Henry barked.

"A touching sentiment," Kelly scoffed. "But that's up to you and her."

Henry and the marshal were both holding their guns on him, but neither could get off a clean shot. The post and Nell made it nearly impossible.

"First off, drop them rods," Kelly ordered.

"That ain't happening," the marshal spat back at him.

Henry looked into her face. Nell was flushed and angry, but she showed no fear.

"What do you want?"

"Simple," Kelly said, turning his glare on Henry. "The money her and her old man was carrying."

Nell shook her head. "No."

"Shut it, you." Kelly banged the muzzle of his pistol against the side of her head. "She didn't leave it in her room, and it weren't in your saddlebags, neither. She don't have it on her, so that means one of you must know where it is. And one of you is gonna tell me."

"He doesn't know," Nell snapped. "And I'll *never* tell you."

The marshal waved his gun at Kelly's man, lying inert on the ground. "These three down and all them folks out on the trail...dead for a few dollars?"

"That's right." The guide yanked at Nell's collar. "So she told you about me."

"Everything." Henry spat in the dirt. "How you took on the job of seeing innocent folks through the mountains to a new home. How you had this gang of backstabbing cutthroats waiting. How you killed folks that didn't have a chance of fighting back."

"Don't sound too purty, when you put it like that."

"How many times you played this game, Kelly?" the marshal barked, his face dark with anger.

"Let's see." The rogue wolf nearly smiled, clearly proud of his own cleverness. "Four times. And it always works. It'll work again too, once I get me more men."

"More men?" Wright scoffed. "You don't really think I'm gonna let you walk out of here."

"I surely do." Kelly face darkened as he focused on the lawman. "And no one-armed tin star is gonna stop me."

Time seemed to stop in the livery stable as they all

glared at each other. It was like the moment before a summer storm unleashes its fury. Or before an attack at dawn. Even the horses in the stalls had ceased to stir. The place was quiet as a church on a Monday.

Kelly turned his glare on Henry. "Let's get on with it. I want that cash."

Henry saw Nell turn her eyes downward and then nod slightly.

"Don't tell this scum nothing," the marshal said.

At that moment, Nell's knees lifted, and she dropped like a stone, jerking Kelly forward and out from the protection of the post.

Henry's and the marshal's pistols spit fire, and there was no chance of Kelly doing any more damage.

Elliot Wright's bullet found the man's belly, and Henry's buried itself in that place where Kelly's heart would have been...if he had one.

12

As HENRY and Nell rode side-by-side up the wide valley, the rugged peaks to the west cast long undulating shadows across the white rolling landscape. The meandering creek they were following was often lost in the encroaching darkness ahead. Far to the east, a forest of deep green fir, glistening from a fresh frosting of snow, covered the rising terrain of the ridge that bordered the grasslands of the valley. Above the tree line, rock and ice gleamed like gold beneath the late-day sun.

Henry would have a lot of explaining to do once he caught up with Marlowe. Between finding Nell and the storm and the wolves and the outlaws in that hellhole of a river town, he'd be able to keep his partner entertained 'til summer.

He glanced at his traveling companion. Turned out,

she was a fine rider. As the stableman said, the gray was a damn good horse, and Nell had chosen the mount as her own. Right now, she was lost in her thoughts as she took in the wintry surroundings.

The snow was only piled up about a foot or so here in the valley, though they'd ridden through some areas just west of Portistown with very deep drifts. It had made for hard going, at times. But in the three days since they left there, she'd never once complained. Hell, she'd never complained from the moment they left that cabin in the mountains.

He'd had a few things to say about that shithole. If he never saw Portistown again, it'd be too soon. They'd stayed for a couple of days until the marshal was on his feet and another storm had passed through. As far as Henry was concerned, every damn minute they spent there was a minute too long.

The proprietor of the hotel had claimed she must have gone out back for just a moment when Bart Kelly and his man slipped up the stairs. Henry had a good idea that she was a few dollars richer for looking the other way. But there was no way to prove it, so he had to let it go.

It was to Nell's credit that she'd gone out the window to get away from those outlaws. At the livery stable, she'd been able to stash the money behind a water trough before Kelly grabbed her. She was lucky no one else had found it before she went back for it.

Henry wasn't impressed with Portistown's doctor, either. They'd had to drag him out of one of the saloons to patch up the marshal. The slug had passed through the arm and missed the bone, making Elliot Wright one fortunate hombre. Henry had seen men lose an arm or a leg from a bullet that smashed a bone. But the lawman was tough as well as lucky. He'd mend.

Before they left, the marshal told Henry to ask for Archibald Macready when he and Nell reached Young-blood Creek. The fellow had established himself as a leader in the growing community and would be a good one to talk to. Henry appreciated having the name.

"How long are you planning on staying in Young-blood Creek?"

Nell's question drew Henry's attention. The closer they got to their destination, the more anxious she seemed. He didn't blame her. She was walking into a new life, in a new town with new people. Up in the mountains, she'd survived on her own, but down here, it would be tougher. Henry knew that from experience. This was the way with people in small towns. She had no kin and would be trying to find a place amongst strangers. They'd have expectations of her, and they'd judge her. Knowing she'd struggle made it so much harder for him. But most of all, he needed to be sure she'd be safe with them.

He exhaled a deep breath that rose like a cloud in the cold air. "I'm staying long enough to see that these folks are trustworthy and that you'll have a roof over your head."

"Neither of those things might happen overnight."

"Then I reckon I'll be staying more than one night."

"You will?"

The hopeful expression on her face made him realize he needed to clarify his plans. His stay wouldn't be open-ended. He had no intention of settling in Youngblood Creek.

"As you know, my partner is waiting for me in Denver. I've got to get there."

"I know."

"You promised to deliver that money to these folks. Once you do that, if we find them to be at all dodgy, you're coming with me."

"What would I do in Denver?"

"I don't know. But a big city has more opportunities for you to find a place—"

"No. I've made up my mind. I'm staying here, at least for a while. That's what my father wanted. That's why we left Boulder. I want to trust his judgment that he knew what was best for us."

"That could be so. The marshal said there are good people in Youngblood Creek. I'm hopeful that we'll find them."

They worked their way down a hill. Henry hoped they'd reach their destination before nightfall.

"Once we get there, I'm going to ask them to give you a reward. I would never have found my way without your help."

Henry shook his head. "I won't accept it. Friends do things for each other with no expectation of reward."

"That's what we are? Friends?"

"Yep. Friends."

"But I've never done anything for you."

"You surely did. The first day I arrived at the cabin, you didn't kill me."

"Oh, yes. There was that." She smiled. "You and Caleb Marlowe. You've been friends long?"

"Long enough to trust each other. And long enough to keep each other out of trouble on occasion."

"What is he like?"

"The man is a legend out here. Marlowe's been everywhere and done everything." Henry told her about his partner's famed history. "He can draw a six-gun faster than a rattler can strike, track a prairie dog through a sandstorm, and shoot the wings off a gnat at a hundred yards."

She scoffed. "I think if you weren't so shy about singing your own praises, you could match Marlowe step for step."

Henry smiled. He had an admirer riding beside him.

"You'd need to pry Marlowe open with a shovel to get him to say one word about the things he's done. And what I've told you...that's nothing. Why, up in Wyoming, he—"

"Yes, but I still don't believe he could ever be as good a man as you."

He couldn't wait to tell Caleb about how hard he'd have to work to live up to the high moral standard that Nell envisioned in Henry. He could almost hear the conversation. Marlowe would turn his dead quiet gunslinger's gaze on him and say only, "the three W's." Henry's favorite things—whiskey, whores, and wagering. But Henry decided Nell didn't need to know anything about that side of him.

"Yep. I'm a damn saint."

"I'm a minister's daughter. Now you've gone too far." She sent him an "over-the-pulpit" look that she must have seen her father deliver to his congregation. "You were saying about your partner."

He tried to make his face look thoughtful. "Me and Marlowe are different. He's quiet. I like to talk. He's a loner. I like to come and go amongst folks. That's what makes us such good partners. That's why we're gonna build that ranch out near Elkhorn." Where he and Caleb could both have what they wanted.

"Do either of you have a woman waiting for you in Elkhorn?"

Henry reckoned quite a few women were waiting for him, even if they didn't know it yet.

"What do you mean?"

"I mean, someone you have an understanding with... or a wife."

Suddenly, Henry knew he was treading on thin ice.

"I can't speak for Marlowe, but I won't marry until I'm settled. And building a ranch takes time." He gestured across the valley, changing the subject. "Look at how the sun plays off them rocks way up there. Pretty, don't you think?"

13

THE DUSK WAS GATHERING, and the smell of cooking fires and baking bread began to drift by them on the breeze. They were getting close.

Before long, Henry and Nell topped a knoll and reined in their horses. Below them lay the makings of a village. Log cabins and sheds and livestock in pens could be seen, scattered across the valley and along the frozen creek. At the center of the fledgling community, a snow-covered mill had stacks of rough-hewn boards piled around it.

There was something familiar about the way the mountains rose up on all sides of the village. The wide, frozen creek curled past the mill.

A half smile pulled at Henry's lips. The scene

reminded him of his father's cherished print. It only needed a few boys hauling saplings back to their families' houses.

By the time they'd ridden down past a dozen snug farmhouses and their surrounding fields, nightfall had descended. Stars were beginning to emerge in a sky marked by only a few scudding clouds. Over the eastern ridge, a full moon rose to guide them.

They reached a livery stable in the center of a cluster of homes, some of them newly constructed of wood planking. An old low-roofed cabin nearby housed a drinking establishment next to a general merchandise store. They appeared to be the only remnants of the town's original settlers, men who'd come in search of gold and silver.

Henry and Nell rode to the door of the stable to find a blacksmith standing inside with the leather apron of his trade in one hand and a hammer in the other.

"Didn't expect to see nobody tonight." He hung up the apron and approached them. "Just about to go in for my supper."

"Glad we caught you," Henry said as they dismounted. The warmth coming from the barn felt good, but the man's face was guarded.

"Can I help you?"

"This is Youngblood Creek?"

He was slow to answer.

About as wide as he was tall, the man had the ruddy face of a fellow who had spent a good many hours looking into the heat of the forge. He wore a thick, rough-spun shirt beneath a heavy vest. Worn brown pants were tucked into battered boots. He also sported the soft wool hat that Henry had seen Scotsmen in the army wear when they were off-duty.

"Yup."

A young boy appeared at the stable door, eyeing them shyly.

"Any chance you can see to our horses?"

"I will...if you aim to be staying."

He made no move to take their mounts. Henry reminded himself that the fellow had no reason to be friendly. Colorado was crawling with rogues and ne'er-do-wells. He was just being cautious.

"What brings you out this way, mister? Don't get too many folks just passing through."

"We got business with a fellow named Archibald Macready. Do you know him?"

A flicker of recognition crossed the man's face. "Yup. You're a friend of his?"

"Marshal Elliot Wright said we should talk to Macready when we get to Youngblood Creek."

"You a friend of the marshal's?"

"Yes."

"Got a name, mister?"

"Jordan. Henry Jordan."

The man spoke to the boy by the barn doors. "Amos, run down to the Macready place. Tell him there's a Henry Jordan here to talk to him."

Without a word, the boy ran off through the snow.

"Thank you," Nell said, speaking for the first time since they arrived.

"Mind if we warm up by your fire while we wait," Henry asked.

"Come on in. I'll take your horses. I don't reckon he'll be but a few minutes."

Nell and Henry pulled their saddlebags and bedding and rifles off their mounts, setting them down by the barn doors. As the blacksmith led the horses away, flurries began to drift down, carried on the breeze.

"What do you think?"

"I don't know."

Henry heard a slight tremble in Nell's voice and looked over. She was scared but doing her best to hide it. He didn't blame her. Youngblood Creek was no Boulder. Who did she know here? No one.

The two stood with their backs to the still-glowing embers of the forge fire. Along the road beyond the livery yard, windows glowed with candlelight, and they'd heard men's voices coming from the bar as they passed. Youngblood Creek was a quiet place. Definitely the kind of town where everyone knew everyone else, and outsiders were to be viewed with suspicion...until they proved themselves otherwise.

They'd barely begun to warm up when a tall man in a dark wool coat and a bowler came striding through the snow with the smith's boy at his heels. As he entered the livery, his dark piercing eyes assessed them and remained on Nell.

"Thank you, Talbot," he said curtly to the blacksmith before addressing Henry. "Mr. Jordan?"

"You're Archibald Macready?"

The newcomer lifted his chin slightly. "What can I do for you?"

"We're here to help *you*," Nell said.

Macready raised an eyebrow. "We haven't been introduced."

"I'm Nell Cody. My father was John Cody. Three months ago, our wagon train out of Boulder was ambushed. Everyone was killed except me."

Macready reached out and touched Nell's sleeve. His face paled. "You...are Nell Cody."

She stepped back, suddenly looking uncertain.

"She is," Henry answered. "I found her in a cabin in the mountains—"

"Excuse me, Mr. Jordan," Archibald Macready said, cutting him off. He gestured toward the door. "Would you both come with me? Our house is just down the road."

14

The walk from the livery stable to the Macready house was short, but the man fired about a hundred questions at them.

The names of the people traveling on the wagon train.

Who attacked them?

How did she get away?

How did Henry Jordan find her?

Where was he coming from and where was he going?

How did she survive all alone for those months?

Nell answered the questions briefly, preferring to let Henry fill in the gaps and answer others.

Macready had an unsettling way of staring at her. He was obviously happy that she'd arrived in Youngblood Creek, but there was something else in the air that she couldn't identify.

She brought up the money that her father entrusted to her. But he didn't seem too interested in it, and that made everything more confusing.

They stopped in front of a new, two-story house. Frost-painted windows glowed with candlelight. A covered porch stretched across the front of the road, and two rockers sat side-by-side.

Macready was still asking questions. "And all of the killers were dispatched in the shootout in Portistown?"

"All of them," Henry answered. "And let me tell you, this young woman here showed unmatched courage."

Macready looked at her for a long moment. "Amazing. Your father would have been so proud."

Leading them to the front door, he ushered them into a central hallway. A number of doors opened out on either side. A set of stairs toward the end led to a second floor. Smells of supper greeted them.

He pointed to a comfortable sitting room to the right. "If you could wait in here for a moment, I'll get Mrs. Macready."

They went in. As their host disappeared down the hallway, Henry paused by the door.

"Remember what I told you. Anytime you don't feel right about this town or these people, we can get back on the road."

"I don't know yet. There's a strangeness about him. Something he's not telling us." Nell removed her hat.

A warm blaze crackled in the fireplace, and a small pine tree stood in a corner, adorned with colorful ribbons and unlit candles. Other signs of Christmas decorations were scattered about. Garlands of spruce and pine draped gracefully over the fireplace. A pair of carved angels on the mantel. Framed works of needle-point with scriptural quotes about the Christ's birth. A large star made of shimmering gold paper hung on the wall.

Standing before it, she thought of the last Christmas with her mother. They always made a Nativity star together. She quickly stepped away; the memory was still too raw.

She paused by an old portrait of a middle-aged couple. The man in the painting was not Archibald Macready. But she'd seen this picture...or these two people. At least, she thought so. Nell wondered if the Macready family came from Boulder. Perhaps they were in her father's congregation.

She picked a Bible up from a table by one of the chairs. A paper slipped from between the pages and fluttered to the floor. She reached for it. It was a letter. The ink had faded, and there was only a little of the handwriting that was still visible. Before she slid it back inside the pages, the scent of the paper made her pause. She raised it to her face and closed her eyes.

Honeysuckle. Nell recalled her mother writing her letters at a desk by a window. From the time she'd been a small child, Nell had helped her, dabbing the page with a spot of perfume.

She breathed in the scent and her throat closed. Tears burned the backs of her eyes. She was back in their house in Boulder. Her mother's presence was all around her.

Light footsteps approached. A woman's soft voice. "Nell...you've come."

Nell opened her eyes.

A woman stood in the doorway, tears glistening on her cheeks. "I always knew you'd come."

Nell stared. The eyes. The shape of her face. The color of her hair. The slender frame.

It all became so clear. The star. The painting. The letter.

"I believed..." The woman faltered for a moment. "Nell, I am your aunt."

15

Henry checked the strap on the saddlebags and ran his hand over the dark bay's neck.

"Reckon we're ready, fella."

The previous days had warmed up a little, and the melt had produced mud in the roads of Youngblood Creek. But last night, the temperature had dropped again, and a snow squall had blanketed the village with a fresh coat of white. The air was brisk and clean, and the town had a definite look of wholesomeness.

Henry was glad. It made leaving a little easier.

The sound of bells drew his eye to a sleigh coming along the road. The driver gave him a jaunty wave as he passed.

"Maybe I oughta get you some bells," he said, and the gelding responded with a shake of his head.

The front door of the Macready house opened. Nell came out, pulling on her coat. Her dark hair gleamed in the morning sunlight.

Henry had already said his farewells to her and to her uncle and aunt.

"Are you sure you can't stay, Henry? You could go after Christmas Day."

"No, I can't."

"That's only two days."

He looked into her face, hearing the catch in her voice. Since their arrival, Nell and her aunt had been inseparable. Their relationship was off to a good start.

From the bits and pieces that Henry heard, John Cody had been motivated to move to Youngblood Creek largely because of his in-laws. Archibald and Nancy Macready had come west with a large group and settled here this past year. Unbeknownst to Nell, Macready and Cody had exchanged letters. With his wife gone, Nell's father decided that they both would benefit from a closer tie with family. He'd held off telling her. It was meant to be a surprise.

Henry gestured toward the house. "Having any doubts about them? That why you want me to stay?"

"No." Nell hugged her middle and shook her head. "They're good people. And they've made it clear that I'm welcome to stay with them as long as I want."

"Then what is wrong?"

"I...I just can't see why you would want to spend Christmas out there on a cold winter road."

"That house, your aunt and uncle, this town...this is your home now. It's time for me to go and find *my* home."

Nell stared out at the glistening mountain peaks. She'd grown up a lot since they'd set on the road. The confidence she carried, despite everything that happened to her, was admirable. He decided she'd do just fine on the frontier, with or without her aunt and uncle.

"Do you think your partner is still waiting on you in Denver?"

"Maybe so. Maybe not. Don't matter. I know where to find him."

"And you two are determined to settle in Elkhorn?"

"That's the plan," he said as a young couple walked by and wished them a good day.

Henry glanced around at the fledgling town. New buildings were going up. Smoke was rising from chimneys. A handful of boys and girls were playing down by the frozen creek.

Marshal Wright was correct. The people here were building a special place.

"Do you think you'll ever come back this way?"

"Can't say. Who knows where our road leads?" He tugged at the bearskin bedroll and looked back at her. "So long, Nell."

She threw her arms around his waist and held him. "Thank you, Henry. Thank you for coming through those mountains. Thank you for saving me."

He held onto her for a moment.

"Hell, I'd say we might have saved each other." He forced himself to sound cheerful. "Who knows what kind of trouble I might've got myself into if I showed up in Denver too soon?"

She stepped back and smiled. "Merry Christmas, Henry. And good luck to you."

"And to you, Nell."

Swinging up into the saddle, Henry touched the brim of his hat and nudged the gelding down the road. He turned and looked back only when he reached the top of the next hill. She was still standing by the house, watching him go.

Thank you for taking time to read *The Winter Road*. If you enjoyed it, please consider telling your friends and posting a short review.

Be sure to take a look at the preview of *High Country Justice* included at the end of this book. In that novel, the first installment of the Caleb Marlowe Westerns series, you learn what the future holds for Henry in the wilds of Colorado.

AUTHOR'S NOTE

After writing the first three Caleb Marlowe Westerns, we found that there was great interest among our readers in his partner at the ranch, Henry Jordan. Since we loved Henry, we couldn't help but explore his adventures, starting with this story.

If you haven't checked out the rest of Henry and Caleb's exploits in the Colorado's rough and tumble silver country, go to our website for more information about the novels.

As authors, we work hard to write stories that you will enjoy and recommend to your friends. Please sign up for news and updates and follow Nik James on BookBub.

Finally, if you liked *The Winter Road,* please leave a review online.

You can visit us on our website:

(www.NikJamesAuthor.com)

HIGH COUNTRY JUSTICE

Elkhorn Colorado
May 1878

CALEB MARLOWE SAT and watched the embers of the fire throw flickering shadows on his new cabin walls, but his day was not done. Outside, a muffled sound drew his attention, and Caleb focused on the door at the same time Bear lifted his great head. The thick, golden fur on the neck

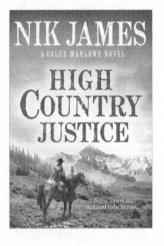

of the dog rose, and the low growl told Caleb that his own instincts were not wrong.

In an instant, both man and dog were on their feet.

Caleb signaled for the big, yellow animal to stay and reached for his Winchester '73. The .44-caliber rifle was leaning, dark and deadly, against the new pine boards he'd nailed up not two hours before. If he'd had time to hang the door, whoever was out there might have gotten the drop on him.

Moving with the stealth of a cougar, Caleb crossed quickly to one side of the door and looked out, holding his gun. The broad fields gleamed like undulating waves of silver under the May moon between the wooded ridges that formed the east and west boundaries of his property. Down the slope from the cabin, by a bend in the shallow river, he could see the newly purchased cattle settled for the night. From this distance, the herd looked black as a pool of dried blood in the wide meadow.

He could see nothing amiss there. Nice and quiet. No wolves or mountain lions harrying the herd and stirring them up. The only sound was a pair of hunting owls hooting at each other in the distant pines. Still, something was wrong. His instincts were rarely off, and he had a prickling feeling on the back of his neck. He levered a cartridge into the chamber.

Caleb slipped outside into the cool, mountain air and moved silently along the wall of the nearly finished cabin. Bear moved ahead of him and disappeared into the shadow cast by the building blocking moonlight. The crisp breeze was light and coming out of the north, from the direction of Elkhorn, three miles away as the crow flies.

When Caleb peered around the corner, he was

aware of the large, yellow smudge of dog standing alert at his feet. Bear was focused on the dark edge of the woods a couple hundred yards beyond Caleb's wagon and the staked areas where the barn, corral, and Henry's house would eventually set. Bear growled low again.

Caleb smelled them before he saw them. Six riders came out of the tall pines, moving slowly along the eastern edge of the meadow, and he felt six pairs of eyes fixed on the cabin.

He had no doubt as to their intentions. They were rustlers, and they were after his cattle. But this was his property—his and Henry's—and that included those steers.

If they'd been smart enough to come down from Elkhorn on the southwestern road, these dolts could have forded the river far below here and had a damn good chance of making off with the herd. It must have surprised the shit out of them, seeing the cabin.

"Bad luck, fellas," Caleb murmured, assessing the situation.

He needed to get a little closer to these snakes. Standing a couple of inches over six feet with broad shoulders and solid muscles, he was hardly an insignificant target, even at night. His wagon was fifty yards nearer to them, but with this moon, they'd spot him and come at him before he got halfway there. It'd take a damn good shot on horseback from a hundred and fifty yards, but they could close that distance in a hurry. And Caleb would have no cover at all. Beyond the wagon, there were half a dozen stone outcroppings, but nothing else to stop a bullet.

Just then, the cattle must have smelled them too, because they started grunting and moving restlessly. That was all the distraction he needed.

Staying low, Caleb ran hard, angling his path to get the wagon between him and the rustlers as quickly as he could.

He nearly made it.

The flash from the lead rider's rifle was accompanied by the crack of wood and an explosion of splinters above the sideboard of the wagon. A second shot thudded dead into the ground a few yards to Caleb's right. Immediately, with shouts and guns blazing, they were all coming hard.

If Caleb had entertained even a fleeting thought that this might have been a neighborly visit—which he hadn't—the idea was shot to hell now.

He raised his Winchester and fired, quickly levering and firing again. The second shot caught the leader. He jerked back off his saddle and dropped to the ground like a stone.

Caleb wasn't watching. As he turned his sights on the next rider, a bullet ripped a hot line across Caleb's gut just a few inches above his belt, spinning him back a step. Big mistake. Now he was really angry.

They were not a hundred yards away, close enough that he could see the moon lighting their features.

And close enough that he wouldn't miss.

Setting his feet, he put a bullet square in the face of the nearest man, taking off the rider's hat and half his head.

That was enough to give the other four second thoughts. Reining in sharp, two swung out of their saddles and dove for cover behind a pair of boulders. The other two turned tail, digging in their spurs and riding hard for the pines.

Shots rang out from the stone outcroppings, and the sound of bullets whizzing through the air and thudding into the ground around him sent Caleb scurrying toward the wagon.

Both of the rustlers stopped firing almost simultaneously, and Caleb knew they were loading fifteen more into their rifles. The man on the right seemed to be the better marksman. His bullets had been doing serious damage to the wagon.

Going down on one knee between the front and back axles, Caleb slid the barrel of his rifle across the wagon's reach. Aiming for the spot on the edge of the boulder where he'd last seen the better shooter positioned, he waited.

He didn't have long to wait. The gleaming barrel of the rustler's rifle appeared, immediately followed by a hatless head. Caleb squeezed the trigger of the weapon Buffalo Bill himself called the *Boss*. The shooter's head disappeared, and the rifle dropped into the grass beside the boulder.

Before Caleb could swing his gun around, the other fellow gave up the cover of his boulder and started running for the pines, stopping only once to turn and fire a round. That was his final mistake. A flash of golden fur streaked across the field, and Bear's teeth were in his shoulder even as he bowled the desperado to the ground. Managing to throw the dog off him as he staggered to his feet, the rustler was drawing his revolver from its holster when Caleb's bullet ripped into him, folding him like an old Barlow knife before he fell.

Caleb called off Bear and strode quickly across the field toward the pines, loading cartridges into his Winchester as he moved. He knew the place where the other two entered the forest had put a deep gulch between them and Elkhorn. So, unless they planned to ride their horses straight up the side of the ridge to the east, they'd boxed themselves in.

Caleb entered the pines, listening for any sound of horse or rider. It was dark as a church here, with only a few openings where the moonlight broke through the boughs. The cool smell of pine filled his senses, and he saw Bear disappear off to the right.

Since the dog was following them, he decided to track to the left.

A few minutes later, his foot caught air, and he nearly went over the edge of the gulch. Caleb caught himself and peered into the blackness of the ravine. The spring melt was long over, and there was no sound of running water. And no sound of any riders that might have gone over the ledge either.

No such luck, he thought.

Working his way along the edge, Caleb soon heard the sound of low voices.

"...got to go back down there. Ain't no other way."

"I ain't heard no shots for a while."

Caleb moved closer until he saw them standing with their horses in a small clearing illuminated by the blue light of the moon.

"Maybe they killed the sumbitch."

"Maybe they did, and maybe they didn't."

They froze when their horses both raised their heads in alarm.

"What's that?"

On the far side of the clearing, Bear crept into view, head lowered and teeth bared.

Before either one could draw, Caleb stepped in behind them. "Throw 'em down."

Unfortunately, some fellows never know when to fold a losing hand.

One of them drew his revolver as he whirled toward the voice. Caleb's Winchester barked, dropping the man where he stood.

The other swung his rifle but never got the shot off. Bear leaped, biting down on the wrist of the hand holding the forend. Locking his viselike jaws, the dog shook his head fiercely, eliciting a scream.

Trying to yank his hand and the weapon free, the rustler stumbled and fell backward into the shadow of the tall pines, pulling the yellow dog with him. As Caleb ran toward them, he fired his rifle. The intruder twitched once and lay still.

Even in the dim light, he could see the life go out of the man's eyes. The bullet had caught him under the chin and gone straight up.

"Leave him, Bear," he ordered.

The black-faced dog backed away, shook his golden fur, and stood looking expectantly at his master.

"Done good, boy."

Caleb straightened up and, for the first time, felt the stinging burn from the bullet that had grazed his stomach. Pulling open the rent in his shirt, he examined the wound as well as he could. Some bleeding had occurred, but it had mostly stopped.

Could have been a lot worse, he thought.

A few minutes later, with the two dead men tethered across their saddles, Caleb led the horses single file back down through the pine forest. As they drew near the open meadow, Bear stopped short and raised his nose before focusing on something ahead.

Caleb looped the reins of the lead horse over a low branch and moved stealthily forward.

In the darkness at the edge of the forest, another rider—wearing a bowler and a canvas duster—was peering out at the unfinished cabin and the four saddled horses grazing in the silvery field. Caleb raised his rifle and took dead aim.

"All right. Raise your hands where I can see them."

Slowly, the hands lifted into the air as Bear trotted over and sniffed at the intruder's boot.

"Start talking," Caleb demanded.

As the rider turned in the saddle, a spear of moonlight illuminated her face. A woman's face, and a damn pretty one, at that.

Caleb nearly fell over in surprise.

"I was coming after you, Mr. Marlowe. But the fellows who were riding those horses beat me to it."

———

CALEB APPROACHED THE WOMAN CAUTIOUSLY. Right now, he was trying to ignore the empty feeling that always came after killing. And even though his instincts told him this rider had no intention of doing him any harm, he had no assurance she wasn't packing a firearm beneath that duster.

"You are Mr. Marlowe, aren't you?"

"I am. What's your connection with those fellas, ma'am?"

The rider tilted her head slightly as she considered the question. "Oh! I have no connection with them whatsoever. I was coming to find you when I saw them leaving Elkhorn ahead of me."

"And you followed?" His tone was sharp. Following six unfamiliar men in the middle of the night.

"I heard one of them mention your name." She matched his tone. "I figured following them would be the easiest way to get here. They did look like a rough bunch, however, so I was careful and stayed well behind them."

He wasn't feeling any better about what she'd done but decided to let her talk. The sooner she had her say, the sooner he could go about his own business. He had more bodies to collect while the moon was still high.

"I must admit, when they turned off the road into the pine forest some distance from town, I got a bit lost. But I heard gunshots and followed the sound. I hope there was no trouble."

Depends on who you ask, he thought. Caleb eyed her horse. "Ain't that Doc Burnett's gelding?"

"Yes, it is."

"Who are you, ma'am, and what are you doing with his horse?"

She took off the bowler, and a thick braid fell down her back. "I'm Sheila Burnett. My father is Dr. Burnett. I know from his letters that he's a friend of yours."

Caleb was taken aback by her words. Doc was indeed a friend of his, about the only one he'd claim as such in Elkhorn. But he'd had the impression that Doc's daughter was a young girl living with his in-laws back East somewhere. This was a grown and confident woman.

Maybe a bit overconfident.

"Why the devil is your father sending you out here in the dark of night, Miss Burnett?" Perhaps his tone was too sharp still, because his dog Bear gave him a look and then trotted off into the pines.

"That's the problem, Mr. Marlowe. He didn't send me. I arrived on the coach from Denver yesterday to find he's gone missing. I need your help finding him."

Caleb had seen Doc only two days ago, and he was just fine. This daughter of his couldn't know it, of course, but the doctor often traveled away from town to look after miners and other folks who needed him.

Caleb cradled his rifle in the crook of his arm. "Your father can take care of himself, Miss Burnett. But tell me, are you armed?"

"Of course not."

She had the false confidence of a greenhorn.

"Was Doc expecting you?"

"In our recent correspondence, I mentioned my interest in paying him a visit."

"Was your father expecting you?" he repeated.

"Not exactly. Once I decided to come, a letter would have been too slow in arriving. And as you know, the telegraph lines haven't reached Elkhorn as yet."

An overly confident greenhorn with an impetuous disposition. A dangerous combination in these wild Rockies. Someone needed to explain a few things to this young woman about the dangers she'd exposed herself to, but he had six dead blackguards who'd be attracting wolves and coyotes and all kinds of undesirables before sunup.

"If you wouldn't mind moving out into the field there a ways, I'll follow you directly. After I finish up a chore or two, I'll take you back to Elkhorn and—"

"But what about finding my father?"

"We'll talk about that after I deliver you back to town."

As Caleb turned to retrieve the horses and the dead men lashed to their saddles, he saw his dog trot out ahead of Doc's daughter.

"And what's your name, fellow?"

"That good boy is Bear," Caleb called after her. "But usually he ain't one to offer up his name to folks he don't know."

A few minutes later, he led the two mounts out into the field to find Miss Burnett standing by her horse with Bear sitting and leaning against her leg. Not his dog's customary response to strangers, though maybe it was because she was wearing Doc's bowler and duster, Caleb decided.

She stopped petting the dog's head, and he heard her sharp intake of breath the moment she saw what the horses were carrying.

"These men are dead?" she asked, her voice wavering.

"Yes, Miss Burnett. They are." Not an uncommon outcome for fellows like these.

"You killed them?"

"I did, ma'am," Caleb replied, stopping as he reached her. "Though it could have turned out different. And that would not have been good for either you or me."

"You took their lives."

That was the same as killing, but he didn't feel it was worth dwelling on. "They came to take mine."

"Are you sure that was what they intended? Did you speak to them before...before...?" She waved a hand toward the dead bodies.

"There's no before in that situation," he said, now irritated.

"You couldn't shoot them in the leg? Or in the arm? You couldn't stop them?" She shook her head in frustration. "Why did you have to kill them?"

When someone opens fire on you in the dead of night, Caleb thought, you react or you're dead. He bit back the lecture he was ready to deliver, reminding himself it wasn't his job to make this woman understand the realities of frontier life.

"Take a step back, ma'am, so I can finish what I have to do here."

As he led the horses bearing the corpses past her, she drew back in silent but obvious aversion.

Welcome to Colorado.

———

Get HIGH COUNTRY JUSTICE
from your favorite retailer today!

ABOUT THE AUTHOR

USA Today Bestselling Authors Nikoo and Jim McGoldrick have crafted over fifty fast-paced, conflict-filled novels, along with two works of nonfiction, under the pseudonyms Nik James, May McGoldrick and Jan Coffey.

These popular and prolific authors write historical romance, suspense, mystery, historical Westerns, and young adult novels. They are four-time Rita Award Finalists and the winners of numerous awards for their writing, including the Daphne DeMaurier Award for Excellence, the *Romantic Times Magazine* Reviewers' Choice Award, three NJRW Golden Leaf Awards, two Holt Medallions, and the Connecticut Press Club Award for Best Fiction. Their work is included in the Popular Culture Library collection of the National Museum of Scotland.

———

www.NikJamesAuthor.com

www.JanCoffey.com

www.MayMcGoldrick.com

FOLLOW NIK JAMES ON SOCIAL MEDIA

facebook.com/nik.james.7712

twitter.com/NikJamesAuthor

instagram.com/nik_james_author

bookbub.com/authors/nik-james